Islanders

Islanders

Cathy Thomas

virago

VIRAGO

First published in Great Britain in 2022 by Virago Press

1 3 5 7 9 10 8 6 4 2

Copyright © Cathy Thomas 2022

The moral right of the author has been asserted.

A CIP catalogue record for this book
is available from the British Library.

Hardback ISBN 978-0-349-01628-3
C format ISBN 978-0-349-01627-6

Typeset in Sabon by M Rules
Printed and bound in Great Britain by
Clays Ltd, Elcograf S.p.A.

Papers used by Virago are from well-managed forests
and other responsible sources.

Virago Press
An imprint of
Little, Brown Book Group
Carmelite House
50 Victoria Embankment
London EC4Y 0DZ

An Hachette UK Company
www.hachette.co.uk

www.virago.co.uk

Contents

Good for a Laugh

Port Soif, 2000

A barbecue is flickering on the dunes below and Port Soif stinks like burnt beefburgers. The boys have hotdogs in the boot of the car, cider and rum too, which they're saving for the bunker party later on. Paul checks his watch. It won't take long before they can get the evening going properly, knowing only too well how Tricky goes about his business.

Becky is already slithering on the bonnet with Tricky's hands on her, all over her, under her. The girl moans into Tricky's ear, her new full bottle of vodka clinking in her handbag against the door keys to her gran's house. She hitches herself higher up on the car and gives Paul a wink.

Paul finishes his ciggy and walks to the other side of the car park. He has seen and heard this routine more times than he cares to remember. Every weekend, Becky gets off with Tricky so that he will buy her alcohol. Tricky doesn't have a car to get around in, but Paul does; and Tricky is the one who gets them the gear for the parties, to which Jean-Christophe gets the invites. Exchanges like this make island life easy for everyone: there is always something to take and somewhere to go.

Paul no longer has an interest in using his ID to get girls, even though they stick to him like iron filings. Everyone starts young on the island, giving themselves longer to find genes that are different from their own. Paul wishes his dad had done that, for sure, his parents being Mahys and Le Maîtres, hundreds of years of local blood distilled into his neck and elbows. Think of the lobster pots you could've carried back in the day, his dad had said when Paul had cried as a child about looking like such a Guern. Think of how rare it is to look like you truly belong to the land where you live.

Not that his dad says much these days, Paul thinks as he stubs out the fag-end on the dog litter bin and slouches back to the shelter of his car. Jean-Christophe opens the passenger door and clambers inside. Paul turns the car radio on.

I'm starving, Jean-Christophe says. Maybe we can go to the chippy before we go out.

Paul nods, but he'd rather not spend the cash in his wallet if he doesn't need to. He hasn't yet sorted a steady job since leaving school.

I feel like getting fucked, Tricky says as he yanks open the car door. Paul can see Becky's silhouette slinking off towards her moped, pulling her hoody over her highlighted hair.

I'm starving, Jean-Christophe repeats. Can we go and get chips now?

Jean-Christophe has thick ropes of muscles across his body. He eats most hours of the day and drinks strawberry protein shakes between snacks. If Jean-Christophe is the brawn and Tricky the brains – at least for sourcing what will make the night speed up – then that makes Paul the getaway driver.

Fine, but then we'll have to get some stash, Tricky says, raising his voice over the engine as Paul scoots out of the cliff car park and back onto the coast road. Unless you've got anything at home?

Jean-Christophe and Paul say that they have nothing that'll get them high enough. Tricky pools their loose change as they pull up to the chip shop up at Cobo. You go in, Paul says, I'll drive round the block and wait.

He's relieved not to have to go inside, reluctant to have to make small talk with the girl from a few years below at school who does odd shifts there. He can't remember if he's shagged her or not. When he was at school, Paul had won favour among the school's female population for taking their virginities, and although he would never have said that he really fancied many of them, it gave him a sense of purpose. When girls smiled at him down the Pollet or in the queue for the petrol pump, it used to make Paul feel liked, but he had been so high most of the time that it was hard to remember who exactly he had done what with. Now he carries an awkwardness around in his pockets. He had always felt sheltered by the shoulder-to-shoulder smallness of the island but now he finds himself paranoid that it will catch him out.

I know exactly what you're doing, a teacher said to him the day he skipped his last A-level exam in favour of the pub. I was just like you at your age. And you should be careful.

Careful not to turn into a shitty science teacher at my old school, you mean, sir? Paul had replied then, earning himself a litter-picking weekend.

Yet on nights like this, circling the chip shop in his Ford Fiesta, his anxiety tells him to take good care indeed. He is relieved when his friends emerge with warm white plastic bags dangling from their wrists like nappy sacks. He pulls over outside the Co-op and they cram inside the car, their mouths already packed with vinegary chips and batter scraps. Paul drives to his favourite car park further south along the coast, ensconced by bunkers and angular concrete Nazi fortifications staring out to sea. Sharp shadows range across the spume. He pulls up the car, its headlights cutting through the darkness just like the Hanois lighthouse in the distance, and puts on the handbrake. The windows steam up as the chips' wrapping paper wilts in their hands.

We could raid our parents' cupboards first, Tricky says. There might be something we can get for free. We can't turn up with just booze, we won't get into the party. What do you reckon your dad's got?

Codeine, antihistamine, beta blockers and Ventolin: anything and everything could be put to use somehow. Paul doesn't fancy going home before they go out but at least it'll mean he can check up on Josie before rifling through the bathroom cabinets.

Paul's dad is asleep on the sofa when he gets in, an empty cider can crumpled beside the dog on the carpet. The dog tilts its nose up towards Paul's palm, snuffling at the smell of chips on his cuff. He picks up the empty can, along with two others from the coffee table that's piled high with out-dated TV guides and crisping editions of *The Guernsey Press*. He bundles them into the kitchen bin, then opens the fridge and puts the two chilled cans from the third shelf into the bobbling pockets of his tracksuit bottoms. He takes a yoghurt and eats it with a tea-stained spoon that is propped on the side of the sink. There's no water in the dog bowl so he refills it before tramping up the stairs.

Josie, he calls up ahead. A stick of light shows beneath his younger sister's door. He knocks, readying one of the tins in his other hand as the price of entry. The tin gasps as he snatches open the ring-pull. There's no answer to his knock so he opens the door.

His sister isn't there. Her room is awash with mess. There is a tangle of vest tops on the floor and various eyeshadow compacts open on her desk. Bronzes, silvers, rough-sea greys. Pencil eyeliners in mauve and black. He sits on her bed, her bow-tied teddy plumped upon her pillows. He surveys the homework folders and textbooks slotted on the shelves along the wall, the bedstead hung with beads from their last family holiday to Nice. Josie had been nine then, pudgy-thighed with a home-cut fringe; now she's in secondary school and collecting more friends and grade As than he'd ever done at her age. The bottles of spirits in the dining-room cabinet, from which Paul himself sneaks finger-widths every week-end, are now emptying at a competitive pace. Her drinking is catching up with his; the one time he queried it, she'd snapped, Well maybe it's time you left home then. He wasn't sure whether she'd meant their dad's house or Guernsey but he never asked.

He sups the sickly cider and looks at the schoolgirl photos tacked across her walls. He resists the urge to phone her with the excuse of seeing if she needs a lift anywhere. She's always fine.

He finishes the end of the cider tin. Drinking and driving

go together like whisky and coke on this island. Besides, Tricky's cousin's a policeman, so no one will rat on him as long as Tricky's in the car. Paul's never been caught, whether at drink-driving or speeding on the Kev Run or phoning his sister while behind the wheel. None of his mates have ever been caught at anything. Paul opens the second cider with a hiss and lets the bubbles fall down his throat. It's stingingly sweet, but it's also free. Another one less for his dad. He downs the rest of it and goes back out to his car.

The Kev Run is out in full force tonight: cars lined up along the short stretch of the north-east coast road, alloys shining and bass juddering from subwoofers. Racing offers a better adrenalin rush than surfing and punch-ups at the North Show, and the number of cars makes it an easy cover for drop-offs. It's more of a peacocking parade than a drag race, although girls rarely bother standing around long enough in the cold to see much of the display.

Paul and Tricky are sitting in the Fiesta, watching the cars drive up and down. Their drug dealer hasn't showed yet, though they've been waiting for what feels like a waste of their evening. Paul scrutinises the young drivers outside: which ones are good, which are reckless, which might go on to take part in the official competitions with cash prizes.

Paul is a confident driver but hasn't fancied getting into racing since he saw someone scrape off half his cheek on the tarmac at the Val des Terres Hill Climb. He'd been young enough then to cling on to his dad's hand, watching the car whomp into a barrier amid the trees and wild garlic. Josie was crying from sunburn and their mum was off flirting with someone else's dad. Paul and his father had stood on the hill that looked out onto the town with its castle and bathing pools and monstrous white yachts, while the paramedics cut off the driver's clothes and rolled him onto a spinal board. He remembered telling his dad how he'd learned in school that the skin was an organ the same as our heart, our lungs, tongues, mouths, the small and large intestines both. His dad had taken a long time to reply, watching the paramedics tape the driver's matted head into a brace. Later, when Paul started dropping Josie off at school and putting fish fingers in the oven for her tea, he would find himself saying what his dad had said to him then: These things happen.

He's clearly not coming, we should head off, says Tricky through a clag of smoke. He flicks the burnished fag-end out of the window and onto the road. He turns to Paul and says, We'd better do a run up the Bouet if we want some stash.

Nothing's worth a run up the Bouet this time of night, Paul says. You'll have your arse bitten off by dogs. Or by Craig.

Craig owes me.

Craig never owes anyone anything, Paul knows. He has never met him in person but he has seen the apprehension in the eyes of younger dealers who work for him.

Craig owes me, Tricky repeats. It was a fucking joke last time; you don't want to pay for that shit again, do you? And we need something, we can't go with nothing. It's not like you found anything at home.

No, Paul admits. But Jean-Christophe's still trying his parents'.

Nah, he'll have given up by now, Tricky says. He's meeting some girl before the party, he'll meet us there. We're nearly at the estate anyway. Only round the corner, it'll take ten minutes. Come on. I'll do the talking.

But what if he's out?

Of course he'll be out, that's the point, Tricky says as he winds up the window. He'll be out on his rounds; all the kids will be having half-term parties this week. He'll be up to his eyes in it.

Celeste opens the door enough for it to look friendly but not enough that the boys can see much beyond the brown sofa and the television that's not far off the sofa's size. Her legs are shiny with what looks like moisturiser and her hair is damp. The flat inside smells of shampoo and oven-baked garlic bread. A baby cries from somewhere.

Craig isn't in, she says.

I know he isn't, that's why we're here, Tricky says.

Paul pushes his fingers onto Tricky's forearm as a warning and says, We can come back.

I didn't know you had a little one, Tricky goes on, ignoring the dig of Paul's fingers, stepping towards the door frame and laying a hammy knuckle on the wood.

It's my neighbour's, Celeste says, instinctively looking behind her as if to check that the baby hasn't been kidnapped from the flat. I said I'd look after him tonight.

So you're the kind of person who can be trusted to know what to do, he says.

Why can't his mum look after him? Paul says.

She's not well.

We're in a bit of a hurry actually, Tricky says. Not much time to chat. He brings his other fist out of his pocket so that his arms form a barricade on the door. Can we come in now?

Paul has never hit a woman, and is as sure as he can be that Tricky hasn't and wouldn't. He tries to picture Craig with Celeste, what their relationship would look like. Paul knows that Celeste is younger than she looks because she was only three years above him at school. Celeste had lived in Forest then, their dads had been friendly to each other at cross-country pick-ups, and sometimes in the school holidays she'd babysit him and his sister. Josie had looked up to her, as any girl would look up to someone older who knew how to smoke and do eyeliner. He wonders what Josie would think now of Celeste's brittle hair and bitten nails, the tiredness of her eyes and marks up her arms. He tries hard not to stare.

What is it? Celeste looks from Paul to Tricky.

Craig wants us to do a drop-off for him, Tricky carries on. He's too busy himself.

Is that true? she asks Paul.

Paul sways slightly from the evening's cider and squints as the strip lighting ices his eyeballs. Sure, he says, as if one word can't make a lie.

We don't want to keep Craig waiting, Tricky says as he shoulders her out of the doorway and pushes on into the flat.

You might as well come in too then, Celeste says finally to Paul, following Tricky into the lounge and scooping up the baby off the sofa cushions before he can get a look at it. She jiggles the bundle of blankets up and down in her arms as she watches the boys for their next move. She says very quietly over the baby's hairless scalp, I hope you know what you're doing.

Where is it? Tricky says.

You mean he asked you to do a job for him but didn't tell you? Celeste replies.

Paul expects Celeste to protest, or shout, or throw something, but she sits down and stares at Paul. She doesn't even get her phone out. Maybe this has happened to her before and she knows it's easier not to get involved. With Craig as a boyfriend, Paul imagines that trying not to get involved must take up a lot of her time.

Tricky begins to open drawers, lift up knick-knacks, shove discarded clothing across the floor with his shoes. He shakes open gossip magazines and scatters cigarettes from a carton onto the tea-marbled coffee table. Where's the bedroom? he says, not waiting for an answer.

Why would you be dealing for Craig? Celeste asks. You're not really, are you?

Paul shrugs.

I'm not thick, she says, keeping her hands busy with the baby squirming on her knee. I just hope you're not too.

Is his mum going to be all right? Paul says with a nod at the baby. The warmth punches out from the electric heater balanced in front of the sofa, and Paul's struggling not to sink back into it. They should've gone straight to the party without the drugs: they shouldn't have come here. It's difficult not to keep an eye on the door in case Craig makes an entrance and mashes them into the carpet.

Hope so, says Celeste, extracting her chunky gold creole earring from the baby's hand. I've got work tomorrow.

Paul doesn't want to look at anything here any more. He considers going to see how Tricky is getting on but he would rather not rifle through underwear drawers and make-up bags. There is the china clink of the cistern lid being replaced. Paul needs a glass of water but he doesn't want to ask Celeste for it. The guilt suppurates beneath the booze and he can feel the night tipping over.

What does your dad think about your new line of work?

Paul looks at her and then catches the shock of his expression in the reflection of the black TV screen. He looks really small sitting down.

How's your dad doing, anyway? she says.

He's all right, Paul says.

I read in the *Press* about him, poor fuck, she says. Even on an island this small you can't get far without a car. How long's he going to be off the roads for?

He's all right, Paul repeats.

Still living at home with him, yeah? And your sister?

Her too, he says.

I always liked your sister. And your mum? How's she?

I wouldn't know.

It's not that far to find out, surely.

She's got a new family, Paul says.

You're a nice boy, I always thought, Celeste says. Did your homework when I asked you, always finished what was on your plate. But I thought you would've grown up a bit more by now. What are you doing for work, really?

What's your point, he says. Paul considers going to the kitchen to fetch himself a drink but would rather have Celeste report back at the end of the night that he wasn't the one to actually nick anything. He used to think that if he drove the car and the others were the ones who did the deals or the fights, then he would still technically be a good guy.

Do you know what it's like to get beaten up, Paul, like properly? Celeste says.

Why are you with him then? Paul snaps, listening out for how Tricky is getting on.

How old are you now? Celeste says.

The baby burps and she jiggles it on her lap, rubbing its

tiny curled back. The legs of the Babygro are too long for him, so that his feet poke out where his knees should be. Bubbles of spit shine on his lips and chin.

Tricky emerges with a square of tinfoil shining through his white T-shirt pocket. He's grinning, sweating from pride and from substances tried and tested.

He'll run you off the roads, Celeste says. Good luck on the Kev when your eyes are bleeding out your nose.

He can't be that bad, Paul says.

That's sweet, she says.

Tricky is already laughing his way down the stairs and away from the estate, clanging his house keys along the metal railings. Paul turns to follow.

Paul, Celeste shouts after him as he tries hard not to turn around and look. I saw your mum down the Co-op last week with her new kids and she was looking really fucking happy.

Anxiety starts to jigger Paul's vision so much that once they're halfway across the island towards the west coast, he has to pull the car into the driveway of La Houguette Primary School with its climbing frames and SLOW CHILDREN traffic signs. It is lead-lined quiet. Paul often ends up here, safe in the knowledge that the police looking for doggers and dealers don't search beyond the cliff car parks.

Give that, Paul says to Tricky, who is thumbing a fat joint between his fingers.

You've finally lost it, Tricky laughs. I've never seen anyone look so scared. If you're scared of Celeste, mate, just wait till Craig gets hold of you.

Do you think she'll tell him? Paul says. He won't actually come after us?

Why, what are you going to do? Leave? Drive to the mainland? Tricky is howling with laughter now.

Paul breathes in deeply and hands the joint back to Tricky.
If he rides out the nausea he'll feel calm enough to drive
again soon. Going to the party will take his mind off it, he
knows, but they've got to get there first and he can feel the
night closing off the unlit lanes like trapdoors.

Tricky and Paul grew up together. They know the local
lanes better than the cracks on their bedroom ceilings and
they know what to say to wind the other up. But what Paul
is starting to forget is what it had been like before. Before
there was porn and vodka and seven per cent cider and
roll-ups and joints and aerosols and wraps and pills and late
nights and insomnia and red eyes and shaving cuts and car
crashes and overdrafts. Before, there had been surfing and
cliff-jumping and Sunday roasts and birthday barbecues
and pocket money; before, he could start a half-term holiday and decide for himself what he wanted to do. Somehow
the last few years have rolled into one bad night out.

What are we actually going to do? Paul says. Tricky is
giggling. Tricky giggles until Paul's breathing slows and he
feels calm enough to start the ignition and let the condensa-
tion slide off the windscreen. Maybe it's the joint but he has
the feeling that he won't find anything hilarious ever again.

There's an old war bunker by the Table des Pions just over
the Pleinmont headland, past the old greenhouses stretched
out across the fields, sagging and splintering in the weeds.
Up the sharp path through the spindly woods where the alcoholic from the now-closed Mercedes garage hanged himself
last year, but just before you get to the fort and the stone
fairy circle. The sea looks medieval from up here, mystic. It's

a good spot for a party, and this is where a lot of the best parties happen.

It's early now, or late to Paul, the moonlight smudging on the slapping sea. Rap music is booming from within. Paul only ever watches MTV at other people's houses but he can picture all the videos, girls in metallic hotpants and cars lined up like something's about to happen. He looks over towards the party. There is a haze hanging over the bunker's entrance from the hash, cut through by strobes of light from the Hanois lighthouse. A wind is getting up over the water, dragging out the musk from the bunker. The smell is Turkish Delight sweet.

It's a fiver to get inside and as soon as you do, there's a makeshift table of mixed beers and spirits, which everyone is welcome to dip into so long as they make a contribution too. Paul adds their rum and cider to the offering. There are people on the floor, slumped across cushions and sacking and plastic bags split open at the sides. Danny Torode is caning lines from a patio table and the sixth-form kid from Alderney is picking out a melody on a guitar. Someone is DJing in one of the dark passageways that spike off from the central concrete chamber. A string of fairy lights is strung up along another, flickering every so often when someone stumbles on the freestanding generator. Becky will be around somewhere with her vodka, so Tricky disappears off into one of the dank channels, tipping the peak of his baseball cap down so that it doesn't scrape the lichen lining the low ceiling.

They don't do parties like this in Winchester, Helen Dorey is saying to whoever will listen. She's back from her art foundation course for reading week, during which she claims she hasn't read a thing but has instead accumulated multiple lovers and some fucking funny stories yeah. There are those here who are still at school, those who have been away to university on the mainland and since returned, those who never left. He's thankful that he can't see anyone from his old year at school. But nobody moves to involve him in conversation at all and somehow that feels worse, like it's because they already know the answers.

Paul considers the booze on the table, aware that Tricky has walked off with their wrap tucked in his pocket. He punches open a tin of cider and picks his way across the muddled floor towards an empty spot, where he perches himself on an upturned keg. He feels lighter with fresh booze in his blood; holding the tin gives him something to do with his hands. He drinks a bit more, feels his shoulders sloping, settles on his seat. In the shadows, he feels less self-conscious. He likes to watch the crowd, and there is always someone at these dos who has undone themselves, through drinking too much or choking or boasting about how much coke they could take when they'd never had a sniff of a line before. The best entertainment at any party is the mistakes of other people.

There is a girl in the corner who's lazing around by herself, her hair draped over her face. Paul has been watching her, trying to work out if she's drunk or asleep, whether she's too far gone, whether she's just enjoying whatever she's taken. He can't work out if it's someone he got with one, two years ago: she seems familiar enough. She still doesn't move for a good few minutes so he goes over to her just to check. She doesn't look up when he asks if she's okay and he turns her onto her side.

It's Josie. She smells like the caustic apple flavouring of the spirit dribbling from the green bottle in her hands. His sister's legs are open slightly and he catches a fuchsia flash

of her bikini bottoms as he kneels down to pick her up. Her
eyes are sticky and struggling in the half-light.

Josie, he says, pulling her top down over her bare stomach.
Come on, he's saying, come with me. He slots his forearms
under her armpits and hauls her out of the chamber, her limp
feet curling through empty cans on the floor. He thinks of
Celeste carrying her neighbour's baby, thinks how Celeste
would carry Josie up the stairs to bed after she fell asleep
watching television. None of the other partygoers turn to
look at him as he hefts his sister out into the smeared morning; it's not the first time that someone has come to a bunker
party before they were ready, and nobody's really ready for
their first time. Her thick breathing wets the shoulder of his
top as he carries his sister over the dewy gorse towards the
car. He isn't angry with her, he thinks; she's just doing what
he's always done.

The sun is rising on the back of the wind. The waves
crunch over the pebbles like crisp packets. Some of Paul's
mates take pleasure in saying that the island's so boring, it's a
heap of shit, it's backwards, it's full of inbreds and pissheads
and can you imagine being one of those people who never
leave? But Paul looks across the sea and back to the headland, to the bunker with its seething music behind him, and
he sees that it is beautiful. He loves this place, not in spite
of the boredom and his angry cousins and drunk dad and
the curly fries served in plastic baskets at the Bowl and the
pride of the Kev Run and all the puny parties, but because
of all these things. The early mornings like this one on the
cliffs are filled with colours you wouldn't see anywhere else.

He opens the back door of his Fiesta and marshmallows
his sister's body onto the back seat. Her head lolls over the

upholstery so he takes off his sweatshirt and rolls it up into a pillow for her. He'll drive Josie home, tuck her into bed. Then he'll get into his own bed and sleep off his hangover for as long as he needs to.

Wait, Tricky calls out from the bunker, emerging from the darkness into the morning warmth. Hang on.

I'm going home, Paul says and pulls the car door shut.

Just a favour for a couple of hours and then you can fuck off with your girl, Tricky says, rapping on the window so that Paul has to wind it down. Tricky frowns when he spots Josie sprawled on the back seat.

We're going home, Paul says.

He places his hands either side of the wheel. Like you're drying the dishes, his driving instructor had always said. His fingers leave sweat prints on the faux leather, gripping hard to stop his hands shaking. He can feel a vein pipping in the inner crease of his left elbow. He puts the key in the ignition and tells Tricky out the window, I'm done.

Craig's found out we've nicked his stash, Tricky says.

So what? Paul says. He was always going to.

We've got to get to him before he gets to us.

I'm not getting in a fight with Craig.

Of course not, you couldn't fight a fish, Tricky says. But you can drive me there and I'll have a go.

No way I'm driving up to The Bridge like this.

It's only round the coast, Tricky says. You could drive there with your bollocks.

Paul winds up the window but Tricky wedges his hand in the way.

Do you want to see my teeth knocked out on a scaffolding pole? Tricky says.

No but—

Are you sure?

But my sister, Paul says.

So what, he says, getting into the passenger seat. We can drop her off first.

Paul persuades Tricky to help carry her up the stairs. Tricky cradles her knees and Paul hooks his fists under her armpits, and they slouch her onto the single bed. Paul tells Tricky to piss off back outside while he sorts her out. Paul takes his sister's trainers off, balls up her socks, arranges the duvet cover over her. Her make-up is butchered across her skin but she is peacefully asleep. He turns her head on one side so her cheek is on the pillow and moves the bin near. He sits on the edge of her bed, one hand resting over her blanketed feet, and takes a breath. Then he slips down to the kitchen to fetch a glass of water, fills the glass right to the top, and takes it up to Josie's bedside. He places it just out of reach so that she won't knock it over.

A car door slams outside and Paul goes to the window to check who it is. No Craig yet. He pictures Tricky in the car waiting for him, bouncing his head along to grinding music and rummaging amongst the empty crisp packets on the floor for a chance pound note. Perhaps Tricky was clever for failing his driving theory test every time.

Paul tweaks the curtains shut so Josie won't get woken up too early by the light. He is aware that he hasn't slept for a long time, not properly. His blood feels carbonated, caffeinated. He closes her bedroom door gently, then the front door to the house, and sees Tricky in the passenger seat of his car, rolling a joint for him.

Daily Specials

Cobo Bay, 2001

C rashes were common on that stretch of Cobo coast road. Last week a lorryload of refrigerated pizzas had shocked the tarmac. Annie had been on the deep-fat fryer at the time getting the next batch of scampi on and she'd had to turn the heat down while she watched the police stop the traffic and clean up.

Today the road was empty and flat and salted from the sea, which was rowdy behind the double-glazing of the chip shop. She could see that the surfers were out getting hit in the faces by their boards, the sky and the waves above and below them the colour of iron left out to rust. It was cold for Guernsey but then it was March. Annie knew with dead certainty that March was the worst month. March was the worst month, Tuesday the worst day, milk chocolate the worst of the three, and watermelon Breezers incontestably the pits. Annie spent a lot of her time at work making lists. Write each thing down and you won't feel the need to worry so much, the school counsellor had suggested.

The school counsellor was also the careers adviser, who was also the PE teacher, and so his careers advice and pastoral care were not things that Annie prized particularly highly. When he'd asked her which subjects she wanted to do at A level and she'd said she hadn't thought that far ahead, he suggested she work towards geography, English and photography. She'd never had any interest in geography, had never thought much about the process of rock erosion. You could watch that happening out of the window of the chip shop if you were there as often as she was, every day in half-term and holidays and most Saturdays the rest of the time. The sea was slowly picking the nose off the headland.

Easter would be followed by end-of-year exams and then even more exams in the years to follow, and maybe university and then moving back to the island for ever. The next stages of her life had been laid out ready for her, and her parents repeatedly told her they were proud of her progress, but Annie knew that not everything was going to plan. She should have lost her virginity by now, but still her breasts were like buns in a paper bag, unopened and left to go hard by themselves.

To help her along, Annie's best friends had arranged for her to lose it to Paul in the car park of the Wayside Cheer Hotel at nine o'clock that night. It would be too cold by then for her to take her tights off fully; she'd have to roll them round her ankles with her shoes still on. She'd worn the thong with the diamanté heart, the pink one from the multipack, and had stashed a can of Impulse in her bag to mask the smell of fried fish that slicked her hair. Just put some effort in, Becky had told her. She was dreading it.

The scampi pieces spat in the oil as Annie shook them over. She'd burnt the corner of a couple of them but then she could always have those ones for her tea. It was only five o'clock. Emptying the scraps tray, batter crisped and sausages burst, she wished she could see what the shape of the night would look like. She was nervous about not being able to distinguish Paul's Ford Fiesta from the other vehicles in the dark car park. She was worried about whether she would try to get into a stranger's car by mistake, not that she would consider Paul a friend. For years, she'd been vaguely aware of him messing around with the older boys in school common rooms or pushing his way out of the door of one house party as he left for another. She didn't know what he did now. Once or twice, she'd seen him picking up his sister at school, helping to put her satchel and sports bag in the boot while the radio bleated autotuned R&B ballads at top volume. She still couldn't picture the car.

She thought about texting Paul to ask what colour it was. But then if it was a dark night they would all look the same colour anyway and she would've used up her one go for texting him. You can't ask him lots of questions, the girls had said. He knows what he's doing, you have to let him get on with it. Becky and Claire had been telling her how she had to act like she didn't care about losing it, even if he put on Island FM when he was doing it or if it really hurt. You wouldn't want him to stop halfway through because then who would ever want to take your other half, they'd said. The other girls at school kept a running tab of who was still a virgin and who wasn't, and the approaching age of consent felt more like a deadline than a starting point.

Clear juice pooled from the breaded scampi as Annie

tugged the plastic knife through the crust. She checked there weren't any customers approaching through the car park before stuffing the scalding fish in between her teeth. She knew it would burn the roof of her mouth but she ate it anyway, blowing through her cheeks as the oil laddered her gums. The chip shop was open all year round but in the winter months it was Guernsey's other chip shop at the north of the island that claimed most of the trade. They were worthy rivals; even Annie's manager admitted that. They fried their chips in beef fat and never ran out of skate. Dads flocked to it like it would save their marriages.

Still, Annie preferred the shop when it was quiet. In the blazing summer, queues coiled down the slipway and well past the pub. She would open small plastic bag after small plastic bag of change as tourists and locals alike crumpled cashpoint notes over the counter. Girls in bikinis clutching plastic pints of cider and black, men with erased tattoos and right arms tanned from hanging out of car windows. Children sunburnt and tired, and all of them angry because they had to pay five pence extra for supermarket-brand ketchup. Her schoolmates had dropped by all the time in the summer holidays too, asking Annie to come out with them after her shift was over. There would be beach barbecues, and blowjobs in caves in exchange for corner-shop Smirnoff. Annie had started making excuses when invites were offered.

Last summer she'd let Kelly's brother on her and his ragged fingernails had traced the scorched line of her scalp, her parting greased with aftersun and knickers silted up with sand. She tried telling herself that it was just sunstroke but she quickly found the insistent movement of his fingers nauseating. She'd had to stop his hand moving further. He was

incredulous: of course he didn't want to talk, he said. Annie
left the party without saying goodbye to anyone. She missed
the last 7E bus and – too red-cheeked to ring her mum for a
lift – walked the stripped coastal path back home alone. The
wind stung her sunburn and the sea was deafening, the only
other noise her flip-flops slapping her steps. It took two hours.
She couldn't stop shaking when she got into bed, knees up to
her chest and burnt shoulders cracking under the weight of it.
At school the next week, he told everyone that she was frigid.
She hadn't gone to another beach party since.

The more parties that Annie turned down, the less her
schoolmates thought to ask her along. Soon they stopped
asking her out to birthdays and barbecues at all, assuming
she would say no, and she'd taken to saying that her parents
wouldn't let her out late. It wasn't that Annie didn't want
to spend time with her friends; rather that she wanted to do
what they'd always done together before: reading horoscopes
and making up spells and drawing their future houses.
Everything had changed now, except she hadn't. The school
counsellor had approached Annie after noticing in PE that
she wasn't lining up for diving with the same lip-bitten look
of trepidation as she used to. Annie couldn't explain to him
that the idea of sinking under the fug of the pool surface was
nothing now that she thought daily about not turning up for
lessons at all. He'd asked if she was being bullied but no, she
had told herself then, she was not being bullied. It was her
own fault if she had chosen not to join her friends in their
newfound interests up until now. If she wanted to belong to
a group of people and stop feeling lonely, then her body had
to belong to them too.

One of the girls had suggested to her that she might have

more fun if she at least tried it for herself. Annie conceded that it might make her appear normal, even if she didn't feel it. Losing it to Paul in the back seat of his Fiesta would be worth it for having friends to spend the summer with after exams, and for the remaining few years of school after that. It would stop teachers asking questions, and she could picture the happy look on her parents' faces when she'd say she was going out to meet her friends on a Saturday night. You've got so many lovely friends, her mum always said to her.

The school counsellor knew that she worked in the chip shop, as he regularly took his three children there on weekends for chicken nuggets and a cone of chips each, and on his last visit he'd made chit-chat with her about her evening plans. She'd spat on his haddock when he wasn't looking. She didn't often spit in the customers' food – and when the manager was on duty would never dream of it, because it was either this place or the garage, if she wanted a weekend job, and this place meant staying indoors in the winter at least – but sometimes it helped. It was the kind of behaviour that Annie's dad would say demonstrated a lack of respect among the younger generation, a condition from which he always said she was exempt.

She would show him lack of respect, she thought, looking out on the empty coast road and the darkening shore choked out behind it. Just wait till nine o'clock. It wouldn't take long, ten or fifteen minutes at most. She would go to the Co-op over the road and buy a bottle of vodka first. All of the underage girls bought theirs from there: the cashier was only just eighteen himself and hadn't made many friends at school because of his acne and Portuguese parentage. Annie had never made friends with him in case it made her own social status even more precarious, but she would always smile at him. He would do anything for a smile but then who wouldn't when they were missing the real thing? She would be out of the automatic doors before she could see the disappointment on his face when he realised there was another guy waiting for her outside.

Paul had already got with Kelly and Nikki in her year. Possibly some of the girls from the girls' school that they didn't like or speak to because someone had once said they were slags. Paul was reliable in his duties and not a big talker. He was one of the only older guys they knew who wasn't a total lairy prick, too busy setting fire to waste bins or getting chucked out of nightclubs after two pints. No, Paul was just a loser. Annie had asked Nikki whether she would be jealous if she went with him and Nikki had said, God no, not with Paul, that was the whole point. He wasn't someone you could get proprietorial about: you'd be happy to forget him. After two text messages and an introductory hand-job behind the sports pavilion, it was all arranged. Nikki and Claire spoke to Annie with more sincerity than they had done in weeks, asking her how excited she was and saying how pleased they were for her feeling ready to do it. It's just about finding the time that's right for you, they'd said. Becky had given her whispered tips on hair removal and what noises to make. How lucky to be a girl with desires, Annie thought. Annie couldn't stop picturing how Paul had a poky cock like the razor clams that washed up the beach on low tide, thin pale things broken open and picked at by gulls.

Annie checked her mobile phone, which used to belong to her dad and so made her feel all the more uneasy for using it to arrange the evening. The knowledge that growing up necessitated disappointing her parents was something that troubled Annie a lot, but she never added it to her list of worries in case her dad found the bit of paper. We can trust you, her parents always said, you're always so sensible. Annie was their only child and her sense of duty to them was lodged between her back teeth. She'd rather go home to them right now and watch a detective drama on the sofa between them, not clamber under Paul and stare at the digital clock on the dashboard until he was done. It was half eight now, nearly time to start cleaning up the chip shop. No texts still. She wiped the scampi grease off the phone screen and pocketed it. Then she took a peanut-flavoured chocolate bar off the stand and pocketed that too.

The manager had instructed her to defrost an extra bag of chips before the evening set in. This optimism for big business was misplaced here, and now the half-defrosted mass was dripping on the lino, leaking under the jumbo tubs of coleslaw and humane mousetraps. It was even heavier hauling the bag back into the freezer than it had been when she'd dragged it out at the start of her shift. Next she would turn off the oil and let the scrim drain away. Take out the J-cloth from under the sink, spray down the surfaces, scrape the scraps into the empty vanilla ice-cream carton and shake them outside for the gulls. Wipe off the specials board, even though they were the same every day and she'd be writing up the same fish fillet options again tomorrow. Cod, haddock, hake, skate. She would likely need an extra squirt of cream cleaner to get the stubborn writing off. She had done this clean-up every night for the past seven days but tonight she couldn't remember where the lemon Cif was.

Annie had her anorak on six minutes before closing time

and felt she'd better wait until the full hour, but still no customers came. The wind was picking up and the pub down
the road would be busy, but it wasn't fish and chips season
yet. The gulls were thumping on the skylight in the kitchen
ceiling, hungrier now they'd had a taste. She turned off the
ticking strip lights and took out the bin bags. She put the
ten- and twenty-pence pieces back into their little labelled
see-through bags in the till, and locked it. Then she locked
the shop door and popped the keys back through the letter
box as she always did.

The road was quiet as she sloped over to the village Co-op,
pausing at the zebra crossing out of habit even though there
was no need to. Although she couldn't see the waves over
the sea wall, she could hear them blasting through the night.
There's no such thing as silence on an island. She did up the
zip of her coat to the top so that she could feel the metal tag
pushing into her chin. She slipped through the car park and
hurried into the supermarket.

The Co-op was sealed off from the noise and night outside, the vegetables and stacks of sanitary towels resplendent
under the fluorescent price points. The acned boy whose name
she hadn't bothered to learn was sure enough on the check-
out, so she waved emphatically as she walked towards the
alcohol aisle with its SHOPLIFTERS WILL BE PROSECUTED
warnings. The shelf was empty where the cheap Czar vodka
should have been. The next brand up would've meant breaking into another ten-pound note, which seemed like a waste
for a night like this. Panicked by the need not to be noticed,
she picked up a bottle of discounted Malibu and paid for it
with the kind of smile she thought adults would describe as
happy-go-lucky.

She walked away northwards from the Co-op and the village's surrounding huddle of shops with knitting yarn and fudge propped up in the windows, past the shuttered-up ice-cream van, the cheap hotel, and one of the island's only curry houses. The breeze had the burnt edge of fried onions. The gulls were lined up on the dark outline of the sea wall, lustily watching as she swung her plastic carrier bag about her knees. She walked until she reached the right spot of gravel out in front of the hotel. The only car parked there was a corroded red one with an A4 For Sale sign taped in each window. £250 or best offer, it read. She took shelter from the wind behind the wine-bottle recycling bank, sitting on one of the large rocks that the council had cemented in place instead of bollards because they thought it would look more charming to the tourists. She unscrewed the cap of the bottle in her bag and gulped down some of the cloying coconut rum. It smarted her stomach but she swigged again. Perhaps it'd make her taste like an exotic holiday.

There was a moon, some stars. The sky and the sea were the same colour mauve now, blurring the line of the horizon. He was late but then boys were allowed to be. Annie started to wish that she had stayed in the chip shop now, where it would be warm at least. She'd forgotten to spray herself with body spray before leaving the shop and was beginning to find the smell of fried fish sickening. She tied her hair back so that he might not notice the stench when he kissed her. Perhaps there wouldn't be much kissing anyway, as Nikki hadn't mentioned it in her own lengthy report of being with him. Annie wondered if he did the same things in the same order with all the girls. She wondered if her knickers would be wet in time for when he arrived. Probably not.

At a quarter to ten, Annie decided to use up her one opportunity to send Paul a text message. She had played it cool and was now frankly cold. She would use proper words and full sentences in her communication, however, to show him that she had some dignity. WHERE ARE YOU IM FREEZING she wrote. She tried going back for the apostrophe but couldn't feel her fingertips properly. She had always held disdain for classmates who couldn't punctuate correctly and now felt the shame fighting with the rum in her insides. If he didn't text her back perhaps it would be because of that. And he didn't text her back. She checked whether she had the five stocky lines of full signal on the screen, and she did. But no reply came.

She would need to decide whether to tell the girls that he hadn't bothered showing up, or try to think up a believable excuse. Either way, she didn't fancy explaining how long she'd sat on that rock, the wine bottles rattling by her side in the bin, her lungs shallow and tear ducts stinging. Should she give him another five minutes just in case, she wondered. But she'd been waiting far longer than she should have done to recognise what rejection felt like. It felt almost too hollow to be real. The only thing that she was certain she truly felt was cold, so she drank some more rum.

No cars were coming. She looked down the coastline towards the chip shop where the only lights were coming from the pub next door. Annie's school friends snuck into that pub all the time but Annie looked even younger than she was and rarely got served. Occasionally, after a busy shift when the two of them were on, Annie's manager would take her for a drink there before giving her a lift home. She was thirty-seven and still paid her husband rent, she said, even though she did all the laundry and emptied the cat litter trays. Annie's manager talked a lot about her relationship. Once, on a shift, Annie's manager had dropped her wedding ring in the deep fat fryer. Don't worry about it, love, she'd wept as the next batch of saveloys went in, it wasn't worth it. Annie hadn't been sure whether she'd meant the value in gold or sentiment.

The moon was misted like a cataract and the path shrivelled away from it down the open cliffs. If she walked all the way now, she'd still get home around the original time she'd told her parents to expect her. She was glad of her anorak, despite having niggled with her mum before leaving the house about not needing it. And finally taking off the polyester thong would be a relief of sorts, she supposed. She congratulated herself on her decision to give up on Paul with another swig of Malibu, and another, and began to walk.

Drunks not much older than her were lurching about outside the pub, salt in their eyes and cigarette ash all over the wooden picnic tables. She looked away in fear that they would recognise her from school and ask her questions. Being a virgin at fifteen was one thing but being turned down by Paul was quite another. If the school found out, she'd be laughed out of registration. She heard a cheer as she went past on her slow marathon home, over the next road crossing and round by the kiosk.

Oi oi, someone called at her.

Piss off, she called back, half-hoping that nobody had heard. Her mum disapproved of swearing. Annie chided herself with the bitter thought that nothing good ever happened to good people, and swore more loudly.

Cheer up. You look like you need a drink, eh?

She waggled the rum bottle at them. It was light already. I've got one, she called.

Come back, one of the lads said. Come over here.

Yeah, come on, said another.

Is she at our school?

Just for one, come on, said one of the girls. We'll get it.

Just try, Annie told herself, please try. Maybe she could be like them, more fun and giving less of a fuck. Her friends wouldn't think twice, so why should she? And maybe they were right, if she let go enough to try something new, maybe she would enjoy it. She could feel the booze pushing thickly through her bloodstream like strawberry syrup from the ice-cream van.

She pushed the rum bottle into her pocket, her hand clammy on the glass, and walked over to the group. She knew two of the girls were in upper sixth but the boys she couldn't place. One of the girls offered her a drag on her cigarette and she took it, feeling the scorch on the back of her throat. Even her lips felt burnt, crackling. She tried not to cough.

What are you drinking? asked a boy with hair gelled in chubby fronds over his forehead like fingers.

I'll have a Malibu and pineapple please, proclaimed Annie.

They cheered at her and she knew she had made the wrong choice. Someone else asked her a question and it seemed an age to Annie before she was able to turn her head around in their direction. She tried to listen and ignore the coconut aftertaste.

How old are you? another of the girls asked.

Fifteen, slurred Annie.

A sticky orange glass of alcohol appeared in front of Annie

and she was surprised to find that she was holding a cigarette in her right hand, freshly lit.

She's so sweet, the same girl said to a different one.

I'm not sweet, said Annie.

I like your anorak.

She took a drag on the cigarette, clumsily finding her mouth with her fingers. Everything was slowing down but they were all talking quickly. They talked about older people whose names Annie vaguely recognised as they'd been at the same school some years ago, and they referenced nightclubs and bars in town which she'd seen the outside of. At some point she was given another drink, and then one of the girls gave her a cider and black, and Annie kept drinking rather than talking, and when she got the hiccups one of the older girls kept saying how cute she was and could she plait her hair.

She's not a pet, someone said.

But look at her, the girl said. So sweet.

Someone started crying then about being a virgin and how nobody fancied them or really liked them or would even want to be friends with them after this. It was shocking to Annie that someone was saying these words aloud, especially when she realised that she was the one talking. There was snot all over her anorak sleeves.

Let me give you a lift home, the hair-gelled guy said.

Maybe we should call her parents?

No, no, no, Annie said. She stubbed out the fag she was holding on the wooden picnic table, a few centimetres away from the ashtray. She gulped down tap water from another glass that had somehow appeared in front of her like a magic trick but the water only made the taste of burnt tobacco even stronger on her woolly tongue. She pushed herself upright and disentangled her legs from the bench.

She steered herself back towards the coastal path, waving no-thank-yous behind her. The fishing boats and dinghies, all black now, clapped on the water as she went along. Once she was out of sight from the pub, she stopped for some dregs of the rum from the bottle in her pocket, slopping it down her chin. The Caribbean this was not. Still no texts from Paul. Luckily her friends hadn't contacted her to ask how her big night was going either. It was difficult to walk quickly along the unlit coast, the path wobbly with pebbles and the seagrass hashing her legs. Dog shit and dirty ice-lolly sticks underfoot. The ghoulish trees of Le Guet rose up high on her left and the sea stretched out on her right, with nothing else to see other than dark water and rocks from Albecq round to Fort Hommet.

It was getting colder now. She stopped for a while by the entrance to the nature reserve car park and found a bench to sit on, forcing herself to breathe in and out along with the lashing of the tide. In front of her, the vast curve of Vazon Bay reached out far in the darkness and she could see the white crests of waves spooling over the stepped sea defences. Little squares of light winked from the bungalows along the headland. She breathed. She started to feel her cheeks again.

Back on the coast road, she could see that the surfboards outside the Vazon kiosk were all zipped away and the day's tide times were still chalked up on the board. Oversized Wall's ice-cream flags flapped one way and then the other, the lurid images of Twisters and Nobbly Bobblys rotating in the wind. There was a police car parked by the slipway, its headlamps and interior light switched off so that it could barely be seen from the road. Annie didn't realise it was occupied until she noticed the trance music on the radio palpitating through the rolled-down window.

The next things she saw were flashes in the road ahead, far off like Christmas decorations until all at once the blues and greens and yellows of the emergency services shone right in front of her. There were no sirens, no high-visibility tape or blockades. People in reflective jackets were moving about quietly and with purpose. It could be a film set. There had been a road accident. She had the sudden idea that it could be Paul. I was ready and waiting for him, she'd say to the girls at school, but I had the terrible feeling something had happened. It was the perfect explanation. Annie felt a rushing sense of consolation that was as overwhelming as the rum. She walked closer, and then stopped.

A big silver tin of a car was crushed against the sea wall and there were stains as bright as poster paint on the tarmac. Heavy black tyre marks cartoon-like on the road and glass splintered amongst the wigs of seaweed that had blown over from the beach. The driver was being pulled out of the wreckage by two paramedics, while a third knelt on the ground readying the kit. The driver looked about her father's age, bearded and tired and wearing a sagging pullover that was soiled with dark splatters. He was whimpering. The paramedics proceeded to cut through his clothes, his chest bright white in the darkness. Annie quickly turned away before she could see any more.

Annie willed herself to keep walking. Two police officers got out of the car that was parked up by the kiosk. Over their shoulder-mics came crackles about blood alcohol levels and previous offences. Drink-driving on the phone again, one said, what a fucking loser. Annie nodded as if she understood, even though she felt like she didn't understand anything about being an adult at all. They asked if she was all right and she nodded in what she hoped was a nonchalant way. She stumbled past over the gravel, her anorak pulled taut over the hidden rum bottle. Other girls got in trouble with the police for underage drinking, not her, she reminded herself. She was too much of a good girl to get off with an older guy in a car park, even.

She was sick as she rounded the corner of the next bay. She took a final sip of Malibu to take the sour taste away and dumped the bottle in an animal waste bin. She sat down for a while on a bunker to get her breath back and stop crying but the chill wind heaved her chest again. She closed her eyes and tried to sober up. She thought about her text from hours ago, whether Paul had read it yet or shown it to his mates with a smirk or whether she'd been given a wrong number in the first place. Perhaps he was in his car with another girl right now, who had seen the flash of the message on his phone and tried to read the screen while his face was pressed into her shoulder or tits. Annie wondered who already knew that he hadn't turned up. Her friends would say that she should have tried harder, she should have said or done this or that.

She tightened her shoelaces and wiped her mouth with the corner of her coat and looked back along the coast towards the kiosk, but it was out of sight now. The ambulance would be on its way to the hospital, the car would soon be towed away as if nothing had ever happened at all. There were no further lights up ahead on the path, no sounds other than the sea. No texts on her phone still. She was not quite but nearly home. She thought of her quiet pastel bedroom, the

single bed with its striped covers and the glow-in-the-dark
stars on the ceiling that she still hadn't taken down.

Before she reached the opening of the lane where she lived,
she typed out a text message to Nikki. I didn't do it, were
the words she slowly clicked out, the predictive text flicking
through the variations in her sentence on the squat screen.
This statement sounded less pathetic than saying that Paul
had stood her up. But what if he hadn't, she kept thinking.
The gritted ground of the lane, the curtained glow from the
low stone houses: everything was sure and certain around
her. She was glad to see the sight of her house with the
kitchen light on. She deleted the words and typed again, I
didn't want to do it.

She could see her mother through the kitchen window,
reaching up her small hand for a patterned mug off the shelf.
She was probably making Annie a hot chocolate ready for
when she came inside; it was a ritual in their house. Annie
could feel how drunk and bog-eyed and ham-tongued she
was. She wiped some of the sick off of the cuff of her anorak
and onto her jeans. Her nose and eyes and throat were raw.
She felt disgusting.

Annie wanted to tell her mum about all of it, about Paul
and the girls at school and the older kids at the pub calling
her a pet and the car crash and the fear that the humiliation
would last her whole life. But she waited in the rustling
shadows of the lane until her mum got tired of waiting up for
her and drank the hot chocolate herself, wrapped her fluffy
cardigan around her and turned the light off. Annie saw her
slippers disappearing upstairs. She waited until the whole
house was dark and opened the door as quietly as she could,
as if she were breaking into somewhere she didn't belong.

A Word for It

St Andrew's, 2002

It's like a warm bath today, she says to the nurse, testing the water with her hands as they wait for the physiotherapist to appear. There is always small talk to make between the two of them because he is always late. The hydrotherapy pool is luminous like an energy drink and the grout has browned around the tiles in huge cross-hatches. There is a steady drip-drip into the overflow pipework as the chlorinated water sloshes into the grille. Pascale's feet whiten as she eases herself down the anti-slip plastic steps. Looking down, her hands tight on the handrails, she notices the dark hairs on her legs brush back against the skin as if they have been painted on.

Turns out my son Kevin knows your daughter, the nurse says, standing up above her on the platform behind the handrail, her white plimsolls squeaking on the damp tiles. The nurse never comes in the water and always keeps her uniform on, which leaves Pascale feeling like she is a schoolgirl and the nurse the sports mistress. Pascale has never learned the nurse's name, even though the physiotherapist introduced himself as Adrian on their first session together a few weeks ago. The nurse adds, They're at school together.

Small world, smiles Pascale.

He's in the year above her, she says. They share a common room.

Oh right, says Pascale, the warm water now up to her chest.

Yeah, she must know him, the nurse says.

Kevin, you said? I'm not sure I've heard of him, Pascale says. But I'm sure she does know him, she seems to know most people.

You could say that, she says. I heard him saying to one of his mates that she knows all the boys in the year above.

Well, she's quite popular, I suppose, says Pascale.

Is that the word, says the nurse with a wrinkle of her lip like she's eaten something unpleasant.

Pascale can feel the hot flush rise up the crimped flesh between her breasts and up towards her neck, a sudden splattering of scarlet in the blue of the pool. How many boys is too many? Are they older, are they pressuring her? Do all of the other parents know? They always blame the mothers, she thinks, especially if they're divorced. Pascale goes to Becky's parent-teacher evenings on her own nowadays, something that hasn't gone unnoticed since Becky's grades slipped in her mocks. I can't do her homework for her, she'd said at the previous meeting, shuffling with shame from one teacher's table to another; no, but you can make her do it herself, they'd said. How am I meant to do that, she'd wanted to ask, taking the A4 handouts about her daughter's poor attention span and refusal to tuck her shirt in. None of them had mentioned anything about Becky getting into trouble with boys too. Pascale considers her daughter's attitude towards homework and thinks it unlikely that Becky could be pressured into anything.

The physiotherapist emerges from the staff door in the corner of the room, his muscles stacked up like toy building bricks above his swimming trunks. He excuses his lateness. He drops into the water with a swiftness that barely breaks the surface, his body suddenly present and ready to demonstrate recommended exercises with the spaghetti floats and rubber weights. He asks Pascale how she's been getting on with practising her knee extensions at home. She nods and answers politely, feeling the water, gel-like, moving between her splayed fingers. She assuages his concerns about her steroids, the inflammation in the joints and the pain she has been experiencing in her knees and hips; these answers trip out of her mouth, one after the other, while she wonders which specific word the physiotherapy nurse had had in mind for her daughter, and whether the woman's son had used it in conversation about Becky first.

Does Becky realise she's being badmouthed by strangers like this, Pascale panics, as she flexes her legs and rotates her ankles to order. She thinks how Becky must be buying condoms from somewhere and that someone they know will have seen her at the counter at the garage or the chemist's, that's how gossip starts around here. Unless she isn't using protection, which would be feckless even for Becky, but it isn't as if Pascale has sat her down and talked about this kind of thing. Sex was never her strong point. Pascale thinks about the single conversation they'd had about periods and how Becky had squirmed and admitted to already using Tampax. Pascale had felt as if she'd failed then, clutching the box of individually wrapped sanitary pads behind her back like a small child at a birthday party.

At times during the session, Pascale looks at her body and is surprised to find that she is attached to it. She looks at her purplish skin underwater, the way her toes look embalmed. The silver elephant charm on her ankle bracelet is floating up like a lifebuoy. She avoids the nurse's gaze but every now and again smiles in her general direction as if to show that she hasn't taken offence at the inference that her teenage daughter is some sort of slut.

At the end of the session, after forty minutes of manipulating and mobilising her rheumatic joints, Pascale hauls herself out of the pool in as dignified a manner as is possible in a swimsuit. She pads along the pimpled tiles towards the changing room where she dries herself with one of the balding spare towels that she reserves especially for these hospital appointments. She peels off the wet costume and catches sight of herself in the mirror on the back of the orange plastic cubicle door. She isn't sure when she stopped shaving her legs, although it must've been before the divorce as she can remember Martin complaining about it. She felt defiant then but now she's embarrassed that the physiotherapist has had to feel the growth. She'd bought Becky a razor not long ago, Pascale thinks, and perhaps that was part of the problem. Why would you shave your legs if not for the prospect of men? Has she been too soft too soon? Pascale worries, pulling on her flesh-tone pants and tugging her jeans up and over her dripping anklebones. She'd drawn the line at letting Becky have a bikini wax but maybe that hasn't prevented her from doing what she wants. With a pinch in her throat, she registers that she doesn't actually know what her daughter wants, or does, or enjoys. Popular, Pascale repeats to herself, unable to pinpoint whether a euphemism is worse than the actual word.

She dries her hair using the tubular dryer attached to the wall. She's gone part time since the diagnosis and there's no need to go back to the office today. Since starting hydrotherapy, she's got into the habit of treating herself to an iced bun and a pot of Earl Grey in one of the tearooms, as her GP had said that self-care was as important as the medication. One of the worst side-effects of the arthritis was feeling old. Today, however, she can't face the hush of a little café with the staff whispering behind the hiss of cappuccinos. She speeds along the coast road without stopping and the milky shoreline flashes in and out of sight like changing TV channels. One of her elderly neighbours waves as she parallel parks in the cul-de-sac. She wants to go over and ask the woman in her beige cardigan, Did you know that my daughter has had multiple sexual partners, according to a boy in the year above her? Have you seen boys coming and going through this white front door when I'm at work? Do you know what they do together? Do they make noise? Have you heard her?

She collects the paper and the rest of the post and dumps them on the side table with her keys. The house is quiet. Becky, she calls up the open staircase, knowing that her daughter will be – or should be – at school. Becky, she shouts, steadying herself with her hand on the ornamental bulb on the bottom banister.

Without taking her shoes off, Pascale hikes up the

carpeted stairs and across the landing to the room with the spray-painted raffia heart hanging on its closed door. Her heart is bumping around her insides and she feels like she's lost control over her legs and feet, which are leading her towards the bed at the centre of the room. She'd bought Becky a double bed for Christmas last year as she was always having friends over for sleepovers; now the expanse of lilac bedding, so obviously the focal point of the whole room, feels laid out like some sort of practical joke. Claire's always staying over, Becky had begged her, it would be so much easier than getting the camp bed out every time, and you know sleeping bags are too hot to properly sleep in. Claire is always staying over, that's true, Pascale knows, but she finds herself yanking back the floral duvet cover anyway to inspect the sheet beneath. No marks, discoloration. She realigns the duvet and shakes out the filling inside, and replaces the toy bear on top of the blankets. Becky can't be having boys back to her room if she's got stuffed animals on the bed, Pascale tells herself.

For a moment, she thinks that perhaps she's overreacting after all, that the nurse's son was lying and that boys aren't brought back here, not ever. She sits on the bed and picks up the bear, which was a gift that Diane had brought round for Becky soon after she was born. We'll need a whole other room just for all this crap, Martin had said. Becky was as tiny as the toy then. Pascale holds it and feels the familiar clumps of synthetic caramel fur, the worn socket in place of a missing eye. She tries to get her breath back. She looks at the clutter of half-drunk mugs and Diet Coke cans on the bedside table, the small glittery hairclips with broken teeth. The photo of Becky and her mates lined up in front of Mont

St Michel on a school trip, brandishing ice creams in a range of unnatural blues and pinks. Becky has carefully cut the photographic paper out around their heads so that the sky is missing and only thin slivers of the castle can be seen in between the girls' bare arms and legs. There are four of them, grinning. Tanned. They are all wearing shorts and vest tops and baseball caps, and two aren't wearing bras. Pascale picks up the misshapen photo between her thumb and forefinger and holds it close to her face, trying to discern from the fuzzy pixels whether the girls have shaved their legs or not. Pascale puts the photo down on the bedside table and opens the drawer before she can convince herself not to.

The drawer is filled with the papered tubes of tampons, both yellow and green, compact and non-applicator, and ruckled magazines whose covers have loosened from repeated reading. There is a plastic pink egg filled with dried-up silly putty, a broken string of orange and silver rosary beads that once belonged to Pascale's mum. Some birthday cards and pens and an exercise book in which Becky used to note down her violin practice, when she still bothered taking the peripatetic lessons and her dad still paid for them. And then beneath the jumble, tucked away at the bottom of the drawer, is a small hardback covered in silver wrapping paper and stickers.

It's been at least two years since Pascale used to sneak into Becky's room to read her diary. During the divorce, she skimmed through the loop-di-loop handwritten pages to make sure that her daughter wasn't experiencing the mental health crisis that other mothers had warned her about. Back then, Becky had written about homework and the teachers she hated, discos at St Margaret's Lodge and what to do for the Millennium. It was almost sweet, laughable. Now Pascale opens the pages and sees the word *pussy* in Becky's big bubbled handwriting and has to shut the diary again, although she keeps one finger as a bookmark on the page. She runs her right hand over the cover, feels where the Sellotaped paper has overlapped the edges to create little clear corners trapped with grime. She reopens it. You shouldn't be reading this, she tells herself, as she smooths the pages where she'd left off and reads –

I said I don't like the word pussy and he said well what else am I meant to call it and I said well like vagina and he said it's not school that's not sexy is it what about minge and I didn't know what else he could call it so I said yeah okay then –

Pascale flips the large-ruled pages backwards, then reads the diary from the start of August through to April, all the afternoons and Friday nights and half-terms in between. The writing is fast, forceful, thoughtful. Pascale barely features, in fact no adults do other than the odd teacher that someone despises or fancies, apart from one mention where Pascale is lamented for not letting Becky have boys over.

Is this why Becky gets shirty with me? she thinks. She only stops reading when she notices the time on Becky's alarm clock. Becky will be on the school bus now, apple core browning in her lunchbox and striped brown seats prickling her thighs above those knee-high socks that Pascale always tells her are too provocative. Pascale tucks the diary away. She knows that she should be angry, disappointed, shocked, all of the words that she usually uses when Becky does something like leave wet towels on the bathroom floor or sneak unopened bottles of wine from the fridge. Irresponsible is a word that she often slings at her daughter during rows;

you'll never grow up if you don't learn to take some respon-
sibility, she'll say. But as Pascale closes the bedside drawer
and smooths the bedsheets, goes down the stairs and slips
her feet out of her shoes at the bottom, she feels an unexpected lightness inside. It reminds her of the time she'd sat
wedged in between Becky and Martin at the top of their first
rollercoaster at a theme park on the mainland, curious and
anxious and bilious all at once.

Becky is going through a vegetarian phase. The ready-mixed
balsamic salad vinaigrette is seeping into the pastry of the
oven-bake Linda McCartney sausage rolls that Pascale bought
from Safeway's on the weekend. Pascale puts the bag of sof-
tening lettuce back in the fridge and sets out the plates, one on
the corner and one at the head of the table. She fetches cutlery
from the drawer, a knife and fork each, and places it beside
the plates before going to shout from the bottom of the stairs.

It's on the table, she shouts, and takes up her seat. She
takes a gulp of water.

She watches Becky as she slips across the tiles towards the
chair in her knee-high socks, tucks herself under the table
and picks up her fork. She looks at her daughter closely but
can't discern any difference in her manner from when she
left for school in the morning, or was at home watching telly
the night before.

How was school? she asks.

Fine, says Becky, slicing up the pastry and squeezing
the flakes into the salad dressing so that they stick blackly
to her fork.

Anything exciting happen?

Nothing exciting happens at school, says Becky.

Oh I don't know, says Pascale. There must be some good gossip sometimes?

What?

Gossip, says Pascale. There must be some of it.

Jesus Christ, says Becky.

You could ask me how my day was, then.

How was your day?

My day was fine, thank you, says Pascale. I had physio this afternoon. Adrian got in his trunks again.

Good gossip, says Becky, chewing through pastry.

Your food isn't going to be taken away from you, says Pascale, as Becky puts down her cutlery and pushes the plate back, empty already. You can pause for breath, you know.

I was hungry. You tell me off if I don't eat enough, now you're telling me off if I do.

I'm not telling you off.

Can I get up then? I'm finished.

Please.

Please.

You could have a chat with your boring old mum.

Mum. Please.

Why all of the rush, are you going out? Pascale asks. Do you need a lift?

No, says Becky.

No, thank you.

No, thank you.

Not even to the park?

Why would I go to the park now, it's cold out?

I don't know what you get up to in the park.

Stop being weird, says Becky.

Stop being weird, Pascale thinks to herself, except she

can't think of anything to say to her daughter that isn't on the subject of boyfriends or parties or getting into cars or how to get rid of stubble rash. She tries to remember what it was like to kiss someone so much it gave you spots. She worries she will give herself away and Becky stares at her like she has something caught between her teeth. Pascale says, Do you know a Kevin?

What?

Do you know someone called Kevin at your school? Pascale adds as casually as she can, cutting up a foamy square of faux sausage.

Who's Kevin?

My physiotherapy nurse has a son called Kevin, she says. She mentioned him today. She said he's in the year above you.

Kevin? No idea, says Becky. What's he look like?

Well, I haven't met him, she says.

What's his mum look like?

Short. Brown hair. Don't know what colour eyes; I'd have to get a closer look.

Really identifiable. Could be anyone, then. That's helpful.

Well, apparently he knows who you are.

I don't know him.

I thought you knew everyone, you're always saying?

Maybe he's a loser, says Becky.

This hadn't occurred to Pascale. Maybe Kevin's just making stuff up about her romantic exploits because he's jealous of her daughter being pretty and popular, she thinks, before remembering what she had read in her daughter's diary that afternoon. She keeps picturing those grubby words in Becky's girlish handwriting. Most boys probably are losers at your age, Pascale says carefully.

Thanks, Mum, I love being patronised. I can't wait until I'm fifty and waiting to die and then magically the men won't all turn out to be pricks.

Language.

Come off it. Is now when you tell me that Dad was actually the best thing that ever happened to you?

No, says Pascale. Because I met him when I was your age, and he definitely was a loser then.

So why did you get with him?

He offered.

That's embarrassing, Mum, even for you.

Pascale laughs and Becky scowls at the unexpected reaction she has provoked. Pascale adds, So no boyfriends on the scene that I should know about, then?

Oh, I see what's going on, Becky says, standing and picking up her plate in one hand and downing the remaining water in her glass with the other. She stacks the empty glass onto the plate and leaves it on the worktop by the sink, not bothering to even put it in. Thanks for the chat.

Where are you off to? Talk to me.

I'm going to do my homework like you're always telling me to. What was it you said that Mr Giffard said last time? It's hard to tell if it's lack of effort or lack of brain cells?

I don't think a teacher would've said that.

That's what you told me. Unless you were just trying to piss me off.

I never try to, says Pascale, feeling the words like food stuck in the folds of her throat, *piss you off.*

Try harder then, says Becky.

Becky sulks out of the kitchen and Pascale pauses for a few minutes before getting up. She doesn't feel like eating the remaining meat substitute or wilted bits of lamb's lettuce. She scrapes her leftovers into the brown organic waste bin that she keeps on the worktop and then rinses the two plates, slots them into the little white teeth in the dishwasher. She rinses the cutlery and drops them into the latticed plastic holder, and the thought crosses her mind again that she is not good at being a parent. She wonders when she and Becky stopped being a team and became two people who lived together out of necessity. She feels the urge to go upstairs and hug her but instead she unwraps a blue and red rectangular dishwasher tablet and slots it into the plastic compartment, clamping the lid shut. The landline rings and she wipes her hands on her jeans to answer it but Becky has already picked up, shouting down the stairs, You can leave it, Mum, it's for me! Hang up! You haven't hung up! I've got it!

Pascale sits in front of the bluish glare of the television and switches on the home improvement show that she normally likes watching. This time, they're in Cardiff, doing up someone's lounge in terracotta rag-rolled paint. They've put a great big purple sofa in the middle of the room. Pascale can't focus on the final house tour that the minor celebrity presenter is doing with the owners, opening the door under the stairs to reveal a WC with fleur-de-lys carpet up the side of the bath and a Louis XIV style mirror that reflects the couple back at their shocked selves over their toothbrushes. Becky used to laugh along with her at this kind of fiasco. It's not as funny on her own. Pascale goes to fetch her mobile phone from beside the landline on the hallway table and takes it back to the sofa, where she plots out a message with her thumb and forefinger.

Hi Diane its me have u ever had a bikini wax? Love :) Pascale xx

Ow no can you imagine why. Put cashews in curry first time fantastic xxx Diane

Pascale can't imagine it. She wants to go back upstairs and reread Becky's diary to better understand how and why she managed having the hot wax applied and tugged away, but Becky is in her bedroom on the cordless, chatting to one of the girls. During the ad break, Pascale tries to eavesdrop on the way back from the loo but one of the floorboards creaks, so that Becky calls from behind her shut door, Go away, I'm still talking!

Keeping the television on low, as the couple ooh and aah over the way in which the design team have stapled fake plants onto a feature wall in the conservatory, Pascale pads through to the small study and boots up the boxy computer on the desk. She doesn't turn the big light on so when the computer is fully loaded, its internal fans whirring into action, the bright whiteness of the screen makes her want to close her eyes. She moves the mouse and pulls out the special keyboard drawer on its rickety rollers, pushing aside the highlighter pens and perforated paper remnants from Becky's homework. Pascale types some of the words she'd read in Becky's diary into the web browser, one after the other, skim-reading the search results to get a broader understanding rather than clicking on each individual link. How does Becky know all of this? she thinks. Pascale didn't go to bed with Martin until after they'd got engaged. Does Becky sit here and look all of this filth up when she says she's doing her history essays? Is she doing image searches for Hollywoods instead of researching what happened to Archduke Franz Ferdinand?

Pascale messages Diane again, asking her about a

particular phrase that had puzzled her this afternoon but which she has now finally learned the meaning of. She wonders whether these physical acts existed before there were such words for them, but presumably they weren't invented this side of the Millennium. She thinks back to the Y2K party that she and Martin had gone to, arguing behind the neighbours' poolhouse before rushing in for 'Auld Lang Syne'. They hadn't kissed at midnight and he never said she looked nice in the new dress she'd bought for the occasion. He'd long stopped reaching over for her in bed by then, saying he was knackered or he'd had one pint too many after work. It had felt sudden when the removal van emptied half of the house but the lack of I-love-yous had become as everyday as squee-geeing the screen of the new double shower. They never did do it in there anyway, and the his-and-hers twin sinks had since become mother-and-daughter's. Pascale thinks how she hasn't had a night out for a long time, or kissed anyone, or felt like anyone fancied her or even thought about her as someone other than a mum or neighbour or patient. You said you'd wanted children too, she'd spat at Martin that New Year's Eve. Perhaps she might enjoy herself better now without a husband who made her feel like motherhood and middle age had extinguished anything attractive about her.

She has already started tapping in another search query when her friend replies to her text, Hiya Pascale you OK? Is this you? xx Diane.

It is me actually, Pascale thinks, clicking the little cross on the web browser tab and returning to her usual seat on the sofa. The cushions have become gradually depressed by the shape of her bottom over so many consecutive evenings spent sitting down. The interior design programme has finished and a cookery competition one is up next, its fast-cut shots flitting over profiteroles and roasted pineapple. Pascale normally follows this one, finding comfort in the confidence of the male chef who tells them all what they could be doing better, but now she turns the volume down on the remote. She calls Diane on the mobile. Diane, she says as soon as her friend picks up, I was thinking, what if we went away next weekend?

You've finally lost it, says Diane. It sounds as if she is eating.

We could go to Jersey for the night, says Pascale. Go out for dinner, get a pizza, get some cocktails. Get dressed up. Neither of us have had a holiday in ages. Bet we could get a good deal on a hotel at the last minute.

What's got into you? giggles Diane.

Don't you fancy a girls' weekend?

What will you do with Becky?

She's responsible enough, says Pascale. One night won't do any harm.

A lot can happen in one night, says Diane. Have you met your daughter?

Pascale waits until breakfast the next day to tell Becky, who almost chokes on her chocolate-coated cornflakes. I'm trusting you, Pascale says, knowing full well that Becky is going to text all of her mates as soon as she walks out of the front door and into the cul-de-sac with her schoolbag slung over one shoulder even though Pascale repeatedly tells her to use both straps. Pascale doesn't shout down the road after her today, doesn't tell her she'll end up lopsided and won't be thankful to her younger self. She watches her daughter slope towards the coast road and then puts the breakfast things into the dishwasher, before darting upstairs to check Becky's diary again. No new entry, not yet.

She uses her work computer to book a sea-view twin room in a hotel by St Brelade's for her and Diane, and makes the most of a special discount to get them a spa pedicure at a local salon. They have tiny fish that eat off the dead cells and calluses from your feet, she reads. Gel varnish can last for up to three whole weeks. She books their flights on her credit card, arranges for a taxi to meet them at Jersey airport. She makes an appointment for a bikini wax, talking into her mobile in the work car park. Just a tidy then, the woman says on the phone and Pascale repeats back, yes, just a tidy, covering her mouth and looking out for any eavesdropping colleagues. She wonders whether she should get her eyebrows done at the same time.

How's things, says the physiotherapy nurse the next Tuesday.

Great, thanks, says Pascale as she slips into the pool, her legs smooth and glistening. She has bought a new swimsuit with detachable straps that can be crossed and clipped in four different ways.

The nurse nods, puts her hands in the pockets of her scrubs.

My daughter doesn't know who your son is, says Pascale. I asked her after what you said last week, and she said that she doesn't know anyone called Kevin.

Oh, says the nurse. Well. Kevin said.

Pascale swooshes her arms back and forth in the warm water, looking at the oversized plastic clock on the wall rather than at the nurse. Out of the corner of her eye, she can see that the nurse is watching her. She tries not to smile. Have you got any weekend plans?

No. Not really, says the nurse. What about you?

Me? I'm going away with a friend, says Pascale. I can't wait.

She imagines the loo roll streaming over the front garden, brown nubs of beer bottles discarded in the bushes. Her nasturtiums will be all crushed, petals bruised with violet streaks, as if they have been sat on, or worse. Fags will be smudged into the carpets and the fruity tang of alcopops will sting sweet in the air. Cups and cans and crisp packets will spew from black bin bags and the hoover will have been ceremoniously rolled into the middle of the lounge, not plugged in but left in waiting like a threat. Becky will be the shouting, dancing, laughing centre of attention at the party until she later steals away upstairs with a boyfriend whose face Pascale can't define. Pascale pictures the strip of red foiled squares that she has tucked into Becky's bedside drawer, and imagines her daughter's surprise on discovering that permission can be a gift just like a celebrity perfume, or a tenner, or love.

Winners

St Peter Port, 2003

The first lie Becky told that day was to Claire. Coming out of the pharmacy to find her friend gawping at one of the shop window displays along the Pollet, she said, You can't come in with me. Sorry.

I can't come in with you? Why not?

The lady says it just has to be me.

Claire's chin pushed forward in protest. Becky shrugged, relieved that Claire wouldn't follow her inside. Throughout their childhoods, eating frilly pasta with ketchup in their mums' kitchens and getting ready for discos together, Becky had thought that she and Claire would always be the same people. But spending every day of their summer holidays together was making Becky itch for space.

It's because it's confidential, isn't it, Becky went on.

Claire twitched her lips but couldn't muster a retort to the pharmacist's supposed instructions.

Becky strutted back into the chemist's and told the

pharmacist that she needed the morning after pill. She was taken into the small cubicle behind the counter, where she'd been given her flu jab last autumn and the meningitis one before that. The plasterboard walls didn't meet the foam ceiling tiles so that a gap ran all the way around the top of the cubicle and she could see the spotlights in the main shop. She hoped that other customers wouldn't come in and overhear it all.

When did you last have unprotected sex?

About ten o'clock last night.

And what is your normal method of contraception? Are you taking the pill?

Condoms had been fine with all of the boys until now, and she was more annoyed than worried at what had happened with Liam. When he'd got sulky about how long it was taking, she'd fielded the argument by saying, Yeah, sure, we can try doing it without, whatever you want. But being cold-shouldered by Liam now didn't seem so bad in comparison with getting told off by a middle-aged woman in a semi-public space.

Becky looked at the shelves of suntan oil and exfoliating bodywash while the pharmacist asked her about her sexual history. In front of the till were stacks of heart-shaped chapstick tins that had been on sale since February. It was the long summer now, exams were over, and Becky had been seeing Liam for three months. Liam's exams results would be even worse than hers. If Becky's dad were still around, he'd have said that Liam was as thick as a brick. He wasn't that stupid, she thought, as he got what he wanted in the way that all boys had a knack for; maybe that was a subject she should study.

Swallow the single tablet whole with water, the pharmacist said. One of the side effects of the drug is that you can feel nauseous with it. If you vomit within three hours, you'll need to come back and take another tablet. Do you understand?

Becky nodded along, looking remorseful and responsible at the appropriate moments, whatever would get the consultation over with quickly. They were meant to be meeting the rest of their friends that afternoon up at the athletics track.

Are you aware of the risks of unprotected sex, particularly with multiple partners? That you could be exposed to sexually transmitted infections? I'm going to give you some pamphlets on oral and barrier contraceptives to take home and read.

Have you got any water so I can just take it now? she asked.

The pharmacist sighed and went off. Becky could hear the gurgling of a water cooler. She ripped open the foil packaging and took out the pill. The woman returned and presented her with the ridged plastic cup, and Becky knocked back the liquid with the tiny white tablet. She handed the cup back to the woman and in return the woman offered her a fistful of leaflets and free condoms, which she hid in the bottom of her handbag on the way out.

Can you feel it inside you still? asked Claire as they got on the bus.

Feel what?

The stuff, Claire mouthed, reluctant to say the actual word out loud in case it made her sound like she'd studied their biology textbooks too hard, which they both knew she had.

The teacher had never said in science class how long it would actually take to get pregnant, only that you could, if you had unprotected sex. The sperm were like athletes, the teacher had said, the fittest one being the first to reach the egg. Claire boggled her eyes to induce an answer and Becky had to resist telling her to shut up. She had snapped at Claire a few days before and it had made them both feel pinched.

Becky turned to watch St Peter Port trundle away outside of the bus window. Rainbow bunting had been strung along the lamp-posts and the railings for the Island Games, with welcome signage and car parking directions tacked up along the piers. The events were being televised and not just on the local news. It was amazing, Becky thought, that athletes from all over the world – the Falklands and the Caymans, Gotland and Greenland, from the kinds of places she had only ever seen in geography textbooks and on Saturday-morning chat shows – had come here to her home to compete. It felt as if Guernsey had become a place of possibility.

I like your toes, said Claire. Your nail varnish.

Sound.

I like how they're all different colours.

You can borrow whatever when you next come over.

The bus rounded the lane towards their school. Becky nodded at Claire to buzz the buzzer, and she did, and they both shuffled off the bus and into the lay-by. They were wearing denim skirts and trainers, and Claire was wearing one of Becky's vest tops from when she'd stayed over earlier in the week. Becky's mum didn't get angry about where they went, unlike Claire's. Since the divorce, Becky's mum had upped her daughter's pocket money and regularly took Becky out for manicures or eyebrow waxes. She'd even started going for weekends away with friends or sometimes a new boyfriend, leaving Becky the place to herself. Becky's house smelled of verbena reed diffusers; Claire's house smelled of plug-in air fresheners. Claire's house had see-through plastic covers stretched over the armchairs and bottles of vodka slinking in the freezer, and Claire's mum was always screaming at her older sister for getting wrecked. Claire had slept in Becky's bed this summer almost as many times as Becky. It wasn't as if Liam ever wanted to stay over at hers afterwards.

A crowd of all ages was muscling its way towards the athletics track. Becky and Claire trickled along behind them, kicking the grey gravel along the path so that the dust streamed upwards in the rising heat. They stuck to the shade of the trees until the small stadium opened up before them, the large metal structure dull and rusted underneath. It was disorientating to see their school's athletics track so busy when term had long been over. They followed the crowds up the steps and through the aisles to their seats, squeezing past families and sports fans and people from a few years above them in school. Somewhere hotdogs were smoking pinkly on a grill. The air was loud with expectation and delight, and the weather was irresistible. Anyone who was not watching the tournament, here or in their local pub on TV, would be down the beach or sunbathing in the garden or strimming the hedge. The seats were searing hot on their bare thighs.

Shove up, will you, said Becky as they chose a bench and slid along towards the centre.

Should you sit in the shade? asked Claire.

Claire tanned and Becky didn't. Becky said, The view's better here.

The tournament started with shot put and high jump, then long jump and 4 × 100 relay. Becky disliked sports, even though the fact made her feel like a stereotype. Claire, however, was cheering along with the crowds, focused fiercely on the race. Their other friends hadn't arrived yet and Becky checked her mobile phone for messages.

Which one would you go for? Becky asked, pointing at the cluster of male runners waiting on the sidelines. I'd have that one, I like his shoulders.

What about Liam? asked Claire.

It's hypothetical, said Becky.

You shouldn't be thinking of getting off with someone else, said Claire. Not if you really love Liam.

I need the loo, said Becky. She thought how Liam probably fantasised about getting off with other girls all the time.

But the next race is just about to start—

But the next race is just about to start, repeated Becky in a high-pitched voice that didn't really sound like Claire but visibly wounded her all the same. Becky turned away and got up before the urge to apologise became too strong. She pushed her way out along the spectators' stand and down the steps into the shadows. She didn't actually need the toilet but she felt she'd made her point now and had to stick to it, so she started off in the direction of their school.

She crossed the main road, away from the athletics track and towards the sprawling school building. The car park was full with spectators' cars and all of the miniature shrubs potted around them had dried out in the summer heat and died. She could hear the chomp of trainers on the tarmac and looked for the source of the sound. Two male athletes in citrus-coloured sports vests were bouncing a basketball between them, marking each other and snaking free and shooting at a light-coloured brick on the wall of the science block in lieu of a real hoop. She sloped closer.

Here, the taller of the two men said, slinging the ball at her midriff so that Becky was forced to catch it. The dimpled surface of the rubber stung her hands, he'd thrown it with such force. Want to play?

She threw the ball back to him, badly, but he caught it anyway. She expected to walk away at that moment but again, he threw the ball back towards her. She caught it, smiling in spite of herself, and slung it back. He snatched anything that she threw at him, however skewed off to the side or low or high. He had the quick grace of a professional and a power in his body that she hadn't seen before in the likes of Liam or the other teenage boys. She hoped that someone she knew might walk past and see them. She couldn't wait to tell Claire.

Are you racing today? she said.

No, we were in the volleyball tournament yesterday, said the second man. The second man was older than his friend, his hair as long as Becky's and knotted in a loose bun on his crown. His skin was glossed all over from the exercise and the intense sun. He gently intercepted the ball on the next throw and captured it, tossing it from one hand to the other. His movements were easy, oiled, practised. Something in the way his goatee twitched made him look like he was about to laugh.

Is it fun being an athlete?

Winning is fun, said the first one. He was definitely the younger of the two, Becky confirmed, glancing at his fuzzy cheeks and soft underarms.

Have you won anything yet then?

Oh, we win at everything, said the older guy.

He threw the ball hard at her and again she felt the

pimpled surface smack into her hands. She threw it back to him and he looped it over her head and into the imaginary hoop on the outside wall of the room where she'd sat through interminable physics lessons. It was a bit like playing with the games teacher at school, or with her dad when he'd still lived at home. She felt more comfortable with him being older. Apart from teachers and her mum and her mum's boyfriend and Claire's mum, she didn't spend much time around adults, so it was difficult to work out exactly how old he was. He looked older than most of their young teachers but younger than the retired neighbours who lived next door.

You're getting the hang of it now, the younger one said. She thought that perhaps he was twenty, maybe, or twenty-two.

Yeah, she replied, trying not to falter on her next throw.

You don't say much, do you?

Becky bounced the ball and thought of something to say that didn't make her sound as young as she knew she was. Do you like Guernsey?

It's beautiful, said the older one. Do you like Guernsey?

I guess it's all right. There's not loads to do.

We were actually wondering what there is to do here, said the younger one. What do you get up to?

Go down the beach. Go to parties. Go to town.

Sounds like fun.

It's all right.

Sounds like you have a lot of friends, keeping busy like that.

Yeah, said Becky. Everyone sort of knows everyone.

I can empathise, said the older man.

What's it like where you are?

Like this, really.

No, she says. Really?

Really, said the younger one. It's just another island.

But like, hotter?

Yes, hotter. You would need suncream.

I wear suncream all the time.

What else do you do?

She was concentrating too much on trying to think of an answer that sounded cool, so she missed the older guy's next throw and the ball bounced off across the tarmac. She ran off to fetch it and sensed that the two men, young and old, were watching her as she bent over. She resisted the impulse to tug at the hem of her denim skirt.

We're having a party later, if you like parties, the younger one said when she returned. You could bring some of your friends.

Sure, said Becky, wondering whether to invite Claire and Nikki and Annie or any of her other mates to what would surely be a better party than what they were used to. They would be so impressed. She asked for the name of the hotel where the men were staying and what room number, and told them she'd see them later. She lobbed the ball back at the older one and strode off through the car park towards the athletics track.

You've been gone ages, said Claire when Becky sidled back up the bench towards her. Nikki and the others were now crammed down into one of the benches in front of them, waving and smiling at her. Liam and the boys were on their way, apparently.

I was talking to some of the athletes, said Becky. Claire didn't even take her eyes off the movement on the track, so she added more loudly, Some really fit ones.

Yeah right, snorted Claire. She was genuinely hooting at the possibility. She repeated back to her in a mock-sultry voice, Some really fit ones.

Becky decided that she would go to the party alone. After the heats finished and the boys arrived, Becky followed them all to the park. She drank from the bottle that was being passed around, ate some of Claire's chips and perched on the edge of the kiddies' roundabout while the boys had a pile-up on the grass. The hours limped along and by nine o'clock, checking the time on her phone, Becky said that she was feeling sick – It's probably from the pill, she whispered to Claire – and slunk away into the sweltering evening to the bus stop by herself.

It was more of a lodging house than a hotel, offering by-the-night deals, always with a plastic VACANCIES sign in the front window. That night, the sign was gone: hotels and apartments up and down the island, whether plush or mould-ing, were full of athletes. This particular site had the look of a Florida motel from the cop shows her mum watched: the plaster coral-coloured in the sunlight, potted palms in front of reception. Hard lines and flat roofs and black rail-ings nailed at diagonals. Becky could hear splashing from a pool beyond the car park. She snuck past the reception desk, the attendant too busy playing solitaire on the computer to notice. The building was carpeted in a variety of piles and colours, from navy blue in the hallway, thick as faux-fur, to heel-thin grey leading into the bedrooms. Becky marched up to the room that was numbered FIVE. She knocked and the door was opened by a lanky man in a sleeveless T-shirt that exposed an array of children's faces inked across his arms.

The next man she saw had a flag knotted over his shoulders. He had the body of a superhero too, all ballooning biceps and legs. Becky tried to loosen her walk into a strut, following the first man inside.

She entered a large family room with smeared windows that slid open onto the hotel's small inner courtyard, where there was a shallow pool and a boarded-up area behind which the wheelie bins were clustered. It was not what she had thought a grown-up's hotel room would look like. There were beer cans and lousy socks and empty plastic water bottles everywhere, and it stank. The twin beds were unmade and there were men sitting on them, on the minibar, on the desk with its faux-leather inset, on the chairs and the floor. One of the men had switched on the television and bronzed bodies were rippling to rappers on screen. It was a bit too loud but that made her feel less like she had to make conversation. She couldn't see the two guys she'd met earlier. A large national flag was pinned across the width of one wall, sagging at its centre over one of the beds, and on the coffee table there was a mess of playing cards and crimped beer bottle caps. In the middle of the crowd, three women in bikini tops and skirts were drinking out of white plastic cups and making each other laugh with exaggerated dance moves. Becky didn't recognise them from school and they ignored her attempts at eye contact. She had done stupid things before, but going to a party where she knew no one and where everyone looked a lot older was making Becky's lungs clump in her chest.

Here, said the guy who had opened the door, picking up a can of Red Stripe from the table and opening it for her, ready to drink. Becky gulped it until it rattled empty. The man took the empty tin from her, mashed it in his hand, and offered her another one. The room began to feel bigger, the music and shrieks of the older women less piercing. Drinking felt like a purpose in itself.

Some of the men looked like sixth-formers and some of them had a meanness to their gaze that she had only ever seen before on the news. The boys her age would be doing shots challenges by this time in the evening, watching WWF wrestling in someone's mum's house and showing off their custom ringtones. By contrast, these men were almost sullen. She wanted to tell Claire this observation. Becky hadn't ever been at a party without Claire. Becky pictured how best to look alluring against the stained Artex wallpaper – hair draped forward and chin tilted back, beer can hanging loosely from her hand as if it was an afterthought – and waited. She tried not to check the time too often.

Becky needed the toilet. She sauntered over to it and locked herself in. She noted in the mirror that she had sunburn on her cheeks from too many hours sat outside in the heat. Perhaps the alcohol was making her red-faced too, she thought, lowering herself onto the toilet and feeling dizzy at the change in height. Someone's hairs were curled on the tiles by her feet, and she put her head in her hands with her elbows on her knees to steady herself. After washing her hands, she splashed her face but she still felt like she was glowing. She decided she would get some fresh air. Returning to the bedroom, she picked her way through the men and the empties towards the doors that opened out onto the communal patio and the pool. Darkness hadn't settled in yet and the low sky was riddled with orange.

The older of the two men she'd met in the morning was floating idly in the green murk of the pool. Beady carcasses of flies cluttered its corners, bobbing with the motion of the water as the man skulled his arms and legs. Her trainers crunched over the dried petals and leaves that littered the tiled patio, approaching the water's edge. He bobbed up to her, chlorine dripping down his tremendous smile. He placed his hands on the tiles near her feet.

So there you are, he said.

So here I am, she said. That was easy, she thought, it saved having to think up something original to say. She often answered back to Claire in this way, a nasty trick when she didn't want to give any of herself away. Now, though, the game was different.

I have a daughter about your age, he said.

Becky didn't give herself time to be put off by this comment. She said, You'd better take good care of me then.

Why don't you get in? he said. It's nice and cool.

I don't have my bathers, she said.

Why would you need them?

Being asked made it easier to peel her top off in full view of the patio doors and rooms beyond. Nobody else had shown an interest in her so she wasn't too worried that they would be looking now. They'd all be going back to their island soon anyway, and there was nobody here from her school to start a rumour. She could feel her nerves adjusting to the novel situation in the same way that your body inches into the coldness of the sea: she was just warming up to it.

Not so sure now? he teased. An ant was already crawling over the crumpled pile of her top, scaling the straps with its tiny black furious legs. She forced her gaze back to the man. The thought crossed her mind that she didn't know his name, but he was waiting for her.

She cannonballed into the pool. She tried not to rasp as she got her breath back, sculling her arms under the mucky water. It was hard to feel sexy floating around among the clots of dead insects, but she felt that maintaining eye contact would help. The sunburn on her cheeks and collarbone was stinging. He drifted towards her in the water with slow, effortless strokes. He was kissing her next, his hands feeling huge on her arms. She felt like an inflatable. They bobbed about for a bit and she kept telling him that she was into it in a way that she hoped seemed suitably adult.

He got out of the pool. She swam over to the steps and climbed out, picking her sodden underwear away from her skin. She followed him through one of the sets of sliding PVC doors into another hotel room, which was just as dingy as the one where the party was carrying on next door. He shut the door behind her. The sound of the speakers bounded through the walls but Becky thought that she didn't mind: it was less awkward than silence.

She rolled down her knickers and watched his face for any sign of expression or emotion. He led her to the bed, where she spotted an open box of condoms on the bedside table. He moved quickly on top of her with the same sense of panic that the other boys she'd known had done, he was just heavier. His hips dug into hers and he made no noise but she liked how he gripped the underside of her arms, making her feel necessary. She felt as if she was watching herself on television, like one of those reality shows; all static night-vision and incandescent eyes; any minute now, the voiceover would start and the narrator would quietly explain the series of events. She wasn't sure herself yet how these could be explained and would have liked someone to tell her how she had got here. She thought that there would always be more to learn about the body, what a girl could do to herself and how and why. Afterwards, he rolled off her in one swift movement, practised as with his other tactics. He yawned. Then he hunched over the edge of the bed, as if he was trying to hide what she knew he was doing.

When he turned around, he lifted up the pilled bedsheet and raised his legs to tuck them under. She briefly saw that his toenails were cracked and his knobbly toes had little tufts of hair all over them. His heels felt rough against hers. As she moved her body closer, he shifted onto his side. He switched off the small electric lamp that was fitted into the MDF bedhead, like a parent might turn off the bedroom light to put a stop to their child's questions. It was not particularly dark in the room, the moonlight and security lights slanting through the sliding doors, and Becky didn't feel tired. She was in a bed she didn't know with a man she didn't know, and nobody knew where she was or what she was doing, and she felt as if her eyes and skin were fizzing with the secret.

Maybe I could come and visit you on your island, she said, the kind of thing that they whispered in the films that Becky watched at friends' sleepovers. He didn't say anything and so she propped herself up on the pillow above him and let her bra strap fall off in a coy, casual manner. Liam went wild for that kind of shit but this man's eyes stayed firmly shut. His arms were by his sides, his body neat and closed. She waited for him to say something, anything, and noted that his breathing had slowed into the steady, spaced-out rhythm of sleep. His nostrils were going in and out like a rabbit's. She giggled at this and ran a finger along the line of his shoulders. Still he didn't wake up.

She tried lying down and closing her eyes but she couldn't sleep next to him. She watched the digital clock display on the hotel phone idle towards morning. She got out of bed and hiked her knickers up, then her skirt and vest top. She pushed her feet into her trainers without hunting for her socks, and the insides of her shoes felt coarse and damp from the pool. She went over to the table by the bin and looked at his things laid out on the scratched wooden surface. She opened his wallet and learned from his driving licence that his name was Adam and he was born in 1965. She flicked past the foreign currency and took the few ten-pound notes that she could find. Tucked behind a crumple of faded receipts, she found a photo of a young girl in a yellow school polo shirt with a mole flecked on her upper lip like she had been drinking hot chocolate. The photo was not dated or signed, so Becky wasn't sure whether this had been taken a few weeks or a few years ago. In the background of the shot, an enormous camellia was blooming against the wall: the angle from which the photo had been taken made it look like she could be wearing the flower in her hair. It looked as if the girl was laughing. Becky replaced the photo and put the wallet back on the table. She didn't go through any of his other belongings.

At the front desk in the hotel lobby, she asked the receptionist to call for a taxi, and she used the pilfered money to pay for it. She had never got a taxi on her own before, and sat in the back stretching her legs. She caught her own eye in the rear-view mirror and liked how her hair was tousled perfectly in the breeze from the half-open window. She watched the morning light shimmer on the coast as it whizzed by, the sand cake-coloured and the water blazing.

She asked the taxi driver to stop at the end of the lane so that she could walk the final few metres back to her mum's house. Becky snuck upstairs to her bedroom, taking the cordless phone with her, and lay on top of the covers. She called Claire when she woke up, suggested that they go to the park that afternoon and get some Bacardi and icepops on the way because it was going to be boiling later. Claire said yeah, sure, the delight of being reunited with her friend unashamed in her voice. After hanging up, Becky only paused for a few seconds before dialling her boyfriend's home number. Liam said yeah, sound, I can come and pick you both up if you want, give you a lift. Becky twisted her hair as he spoke and she could smell the chlorine in it.

In the bathroom, she smoothed some of her mum's expensive moisturiser over the prickling redness on her chin and brushed her teeth. She padded down the stairs to the kitchen, where her mum was pressing bread triangles down into the Breville for cheese and ham toasties. She told herself that from now on she would only do what she wanted, and told her mum that she'd had a right laugh sleeping over at Claire's the night before. She recounted her alibi with brio and her mum grinned and said, What are you two like? Becky grinned too. That was the thing with lying, with life, with all of it: you could just make it up as you went along.

Miss Guernsey

Guernsey Airport, 2003

Your face, says Kat.

Eva wipes the dribble from her chin and looks out of the window. The aeroplane isn't moving. In fact, the plane hasn't moved at all since she'd first shut her eyes, the citrus lights of the Guernsey runway still shining in the drizzle. She looks up into a face that is far too close to her own. She slept badly the night before, worrying about the trip, so she had fallen asleep straight after settling into her seat.

Have you got like a problem or something because you've been snoring like a, like a, Kat goes on. She flicks the remaining contents of a bag of peanuts into her mouth and then tears open the foil to lick the flavoured dust inside. Like a pig, she says finally. I never clocked that about you before. A pig, yeah.

There's fog, explains Kat with a nod at the window.

There is often fog here, descending upon the island like an unwelcome relative in the school holidays. It's considered a local miracle if you can catch a flight connection from the mainland and it's not worth booking weekends away from November till March; you'd be a fool to leave it to Christmas Eve to fly home for the festivities. And yet, perhaps because she has never flown by herself before, Eva hadn't anticipated the problem of bad weather in August. She straightens up in her seat, her neck cricked from where she's slept on her headphones. It's hard not to resent the feeling that nothing like this would happen on the mainland. Now she will have to make small talk with her ex-classmate for the length of the flight as well as the extra time it'll take for the fog to clear up.

How long have we been here for?

It's half two, says Kat.

It's customary for the staff working on the Channel Island flight check-in desks to seat single travellers of the same age together, assuming that they'll know each other and appreciate the familiar company. Fly to or from Guernsey at Christmas or Easter or for Liberation Day, and you'd be 12A and they'd be 12B. Eva's known Kat since they were eleven. They're not friends.

You can have my *Cosmo* if you want, says Kat.

Eva glances at the magazine with suspicion.

I didn't realise you were such a virgin, Kat laughs. It's the same claggy laugh she'd had when she had called Eva poor in front of the whole class during a camping trip to La Bailloterie, on discovering that Eva had only brought one jumper to wear for the whole week-long trip. It hadn't mattered that Kat was the one who lived in States housing, when she was controlling the crowd. Eva had since scrutinised which food brands her parents were buying, whether Safeway's own soft-scoop or Viennetta. Her parents had frowned when she'd asked them for more pocket money and Eva was told that she ought to consider herself lucky, some children didn't get any. Kat could make her believe anything about herself, so it seemed. Eva scrunches herself further into her seat.

Where are you going? says Kat.

I'm just getting comfy.

I meant, like, on the plane.

I'm starting my gap year, replies Eva.

Oh yeah? Kat's jaw protrudes as she tenses the muscles in her mouth. Where are you doing that then?

Brazil, says Eva. The two syllables sound ruder, sharper, more puffed out in the middle and whiter in the teeth than she had intended. She had wanted to sound confident; she hadn't wanted to see Kat blink like she'd caught lemon juice in her eye. They might not be sitting in the upper-sixth common room, surrounded by orange peel and empty crisp bags, but Kat could still start a rumour about Eva as easily as lighting up a fag. Kat has a lot of friends when she needs them. Eva doesn't wish to pique her interest.

What are you doing there then, Kat says in a tone too flat for a question.

Just travelling around. Seeing places, stuff.

On your own?

Yeah.

Kat moves her chin ever so slightly in a small nod. For how long?

Until next August.

Good riddance, eh.

Eva looks away out of the small oval window to see men in high-visibility jackets thrashing their arms about. One is pushing a long line of trolleys across the tarmac towards the terminal building. The airport viewing gallery is dotted with people and Eva wonders if her mum will be up there, waiting and watching. It had shocked Eva to see her mum crying when they said goodbye. Facing the other way from Kat now, pretending to be interested in the mild flurry of activity outside, Eva looks intently at the final few suitcases being lobbed into the hold.

For fuck's sake, I'm just joking, says Kat. You don't need to cry about it.

Eva wipes her nose on the gnawed cuff of her hoody. She suppresses a big gulp as if she'd been hit by a wave at sea. The plane starts to whine and rumble, and the men on the runway outside begin to back away in preparation for take-off.

You're like my sister, she's a right crybaby too, says Kat. You know my sister? Claire? She reckons she's going to enter Miss Guernsey at the South Show, can you imagine? I wasn't going to enter myself but if she thinks she's fit enough, then why shouldn't I? It'll be worth it just to see her face. She's going to go mental. It'll be great.

The coastal shows and fêtes and public holidays tell the time on the island like clockwork, and Eva wonders how she will mark the months ahead of her. She cannot think of a summer when she hasn't been to the South Show, laughing at the entries in the vegetable tents and stuffing gritty candy-floss in her mouth. She had booked her plane tickets with the certainty that all of the things she was leaving behind were ones she had outgrown; now she questions how she could have grown up without them.

You don't say a lot, do you, says Kat.

Eva shrugs. She focuses on the brightly coloured safety card that's tucked into the seat pocket in front of her. An outlined woman in a blue skirt suit is removing her high heels as she prepares to bounce down the emergency slide. Her mouth is perfect and there is no fear in the character's face. She is smiling with a whistle in her manicured hand.

Please ensure that your seat belts are fastened and your tray tables are upright in preparation for take-off, the Tannoy announces.

About time, Kat says as the cabin lights dim and the plane's engines reverberate louder and louder. I wonder if they'll bring out the drinks again. I only got one the first time round, I could do with another. You should have one.

Thanks but I'm all right, says Eva.

You don't look it. Hiya, shouts Kat at the air hostess who is placing a garish lifejacket over her head for the real-time safety demonstration. Eva sees how the hostess's make-up looks just like the illustrated version. Can we have some drinks when you're done?

Kat presents her ID to the hostess as if she's giving her the middle finger. Kat gets them two vodka tonics and one miniature bottle of Chardonnay. She unscrews the wine first, drinks it down like a bottle of water after a netball game, and then rescrews the cap and sets it down next to the plastic cup of bubbling vodka.

Go on, Kat tells her, pushing the second vodka tonic closer to Eva so that a few drops jolt on to the frilled circular serviette.

Eva glances around at the other passengers who are tending to their toddlers and scanning the oversized pink pages of the financial newspapers. Nobody seems to be witnessing the peer pressure. Eva takes a sip. It is more bitter than she had expected and she winces at the taste. She has only drunk alcopops and fruity liqueurs before, has long avoided the heavier vodka and gin and rum of the bus parties and pub crawls.

Lightweight, says Kat.

Eva takes another sip and feels the bubbles pop along her jaw and ears as the plane climbs higher into the sky.

I said stop being a lightweight, says Kat, nudging the bottom of Eva's glass so that Eva is forced to down a big gulp. You'd better get used to drinking if you're going on a gap year. Surprised your parents are letting you go at all. Have you even been away on your own before?

No.

Not on a plane on your own neither, eh?

No, admits Eva.

I thought so. Kat downs the rest of her drink, crumples the plastic cup and pushes her tray table back up into the seat in front. She takes off her denim jacket as if she is too hot in spite of the sluice of air conditioning. She says, I've been flying on my own for years. I do this trip every few months. Not that many people know this about me, says Kat, but I've got a rare heart condition. I normally get the red-eye flight over so I can go to Topshop when it opens before going to the hospital for an appointment afterwards. The one in Jersey doesn't do half the stuff they stock on Oxford Street and there are always scouts looking for models. There was one guy last year there who told me I could be like Gisele, if I grow my hair out.

Eva tries to picture what Gisele looks like. She supposes that Kat does have that quality that models have, in that it is hard to stop looking at her. She's always doing something with a sleight of hand, probably so she can nick something off you or hit you while you're distracted. Eva watches Kat fold up the foil packet from the peanuts into a thin rectangular strip, then fold it over in half, and again, and tuck the ends in so that it makes a neat silver square. Kat then throws the square on the floor of the aisle.

The States pay for my flights so it's sort of like a free shopping trip every six months, Kat is saying. And it's way cheaper to buy stuff there than getting it delivered, so.

Do you not get scared, though? asks Eva, looking at the small silver speck discarded on the navy aeroplane carpet.

You what?

Nothing. Sorry.

What did you say?

Eva can still feel the tonic water pipping in her ears. She is glad at least that Kat is on her own and not surrounded by her usual gang. She tells herself that nothing very bad can happen to her in public like this. There would be witnesses. Eva eventually repeats, Do you not get scared?

Of flying?

Of going to hospital?

Get you, Kat says. I think that's the first real question you've ever asked me.

Oh.

Apart from, why are you being so mean to me?

Sorry.

I'm so sorry, Kat says in a pretend whine. Can't you take a joke?

Sorry.

Come on. Why do you want to know that?

I don't know.

You don't know why you've asked me your first question in the whole time we've known each other. Why are you being such a pussy?

I guess I just can't picture you being scared.

Why can't you picture me being scared?

Because everyone's scared of you.

Including you?

I guess so.

What've I ever done to you?

Eva can't think of anything to say that won't piss her off so she shrugs.

Fine. Here's something, says Kat eventually, leaning over. I'm absolutely terrified of needles. I have to look away every single time. Have done for years. But you've just got to get on with it, eh?

Eva tries not to raise an eyebrow when Kat uses the word echocardiogram, as she can't remember Kat ever being able to successfully read aloud from the set text in any of the English classes they had sat in together. Eva concedes that Kat doesn't sound so stupid when she isn't being forced to recite someone else's words. Eva isn't sure whether this makes Kat more or less intimidating. She peeks out of the window to see that the plane is approaching the jigsaw coast of the mainland, noting the dots of fishing boats and yachts and the whorls of waves above submerged clusters of rocks. There are twenty minutes left until they land at Gatwick, which will mean having to follow the signs for connecting flights and find her way to check-in. She wonders how often it will be acceptable to call home from South America. She should have checked the time difference for when she lands at São Paulo. Time suddenly seems to be ramming forward.

You were the one who asked me a question. Are you even listening?

The plane bumps down onto the runway. Kat flicks open her seat belt before the warning lights go off, and reaches for her tasselled suede handbag from under the seat in front. She stands up, waiting, her thick arms hanging over the headrest.

Your bag in the hold, is it?

Yes, says Eva. At least she will be able to hang back by herself, she thinks, giving herself time to calm down and find a payphone and check the travel confirmation print-outs in the plastic wallet in her backpack.

I'd wait with you but I've got to crack on, says Kat.

The wind snatches away the rest of Kat's words as they wrestle down the disembarkation ladder with their things. The fog has dwindled to a delicate, gauzy mist in the mainland air. It is a lot colder here than in Guernsey, the heat of the school holidays having been all Eva has known for the past few months, and she is surprised by the jolt of her own teeth clattering.

Do you want this? Kat offers, holding out her denim jacket.

No, thanks.

Come on. It'll be nerves, Kat goes, holding up the shoulders and twisting round to help Eva put her arms through the armholes. My little sister gets cold when she gets tired or nervous, reckon she's got half my wardrobe by now. Anyway, the weather will be scorchio when you get there. You'll get to show off your new tattoos then.

My what? Eva says.

I thought everyone who goes travelling gets a tattoo, says

Kat, tilting her head on one side to look at her. What will you get? A big bleeding heart with MUMMY written inside it? Or maybe an address label like you're Paddington fucking Bear – I'm lost, please send me home?

Eva buttons up Kat's jacket over her hoody so that her chest is tight with the layers of fabric.

Pretend to look excited at least, says Kat. Cheer up. You're going to be on a banana boat with a load of fits and I'm going to be at the Vale Earth Fair getting pissed with a bunch of twats from our school.

Eva has not considered that Kat might be jealous of her. The strangeness of the thought takes her out of her worries. She looks at Kat's expression and tries to discern whether the knot in her eyebrows denotes disgust or envy. Eva hasn't told anyone but she is only able to afford this trip because her granny died; her summer job would have barely covered the long-haul flights. Kat probably won't ever get to go on a trip like this, Eva realises, and until now she had never thought that she and Kat might actually want to do the same thing.

Eva replies, Don't worry, I probably won't go on a banana boat.

Don't be such a fucking loser, says Kat. If you don't come back next summer saying you got off with someone on a banana boat, then I don't want to see your smug face again. If you don't want to do it for yourself, do it for me.

Eva smiles.

They traipse through a crochet of corridors towards the baggage reclaim signs. Sniffer dogs and bored-looking customs officers are crowded around every door. The walls display a series of posters with aggressive anti-drugs slogans and suggested helpline numbers. The signs for FLIGHT CONNECTIONS point in a different direction to passport control. She turns to ask Kat if she wants her jacket back but Kat has already camouflaged into the crowds of passengers queueing up for identity checks. Eva checks the sign again to make sure she's going in the right direction, and turns around for a final look at the arrivals area to see that Kat is giving her the V sign. Eva laughs with something like relief. Then Kat puts her tongue through the V and Eva twists away, wondering whether she feels upset only because Kat making a rude gesture will be her final memory of home for the next year.

On late nights lit up by stinking fridges in youth hostels or mornings waiting in bus shelters with her arms circled around her backpack, Eva feels a terrible longing to be home. This itself does not surprise her; rather, she is surprised that she manages to override this feeling and stay on her planned route, visiting the towns that she has pre-marked in her guidebook, bussing between hostels. During the lengthy time that she spends travelling on her own, she tries to rehearse what she will say to people when she is asked about the specifics of her gap year. It was amazing, she would say, you should've seen the sunsets. The marine turtles nesting on the beach were so cute. The bars and the people she'd met, all the music, plus one day she'd run into a group of young people who got a ferry to Uruguay and they camped on the beaches. She would omit the snarls of the stray dogs that frightened her, the scabbed-over bug bites, the constant drinking and the dank hangovers in the heat.

Kat had been right about all the boozing, Eva often thinks, as she is jollied into necking shots of vodka or mescal. When strangers goad Eva into trying coke in the hostel toilet and teach her how to flick over the inner glass of a Jägerbomb as if it were a fly, she is reminded of Kat. In the way that she sees taxi drivers wearing rosary beads and other gap-year students wearing anarchy symbols and St Christopher's medals, so Eva begins to wear her imagined version of Kat as an amulet. It is a charm against the liquored smiles and bad breath and stained mattresses and spiders that she encounters throughout her time alone, and all the time that she feels lonely in the company of others.

Eva cannot fully shake the self-consciousness that she has developed from growing up on a small island but she emulates Kat's bolshiness where she can. It is slow going. She finds herself having sex with a man who she doesn't particularly like, a Philadelphia undergraduate called Dean with incisors as thin and tawny as a hamster's, but she calms herself down from crying by telling herself that Kat wouldn't care. Kat would not give a shit, she repeats to herself, over and over. She emails her mum once a week, and uses her remaining minutes at internet cafés to look up photos of Guernsey. Portinfer, Port Soif, Vazon, Fermain, Cobo, Petit Bot, Petit Port. It looks just like another place to visit in the photos: like the ones in her guidebook. She enjoys it when other travellers ask her where she is from, and she has to explain it in detail to their squinting, scowling faces. It's a tiny island in the middle of the English Channel but closer to France, but yeah, it's not French, no. It takes her time to get this patter down but she does, and she learns to banter and sigh and say the opposite to what she means in order to have company or protection when she needs it most.

*

When she arrives home in Guernsey, Eva's mother can't believe how blonde her hair is and how her eyes seem bluer against her nutmeg tan. Eva can't believe how small the airport feels and how dated the popstar posters on her bedroom walls look. She rips everything down and begins to pack two large suitcases for university. She only has a few weeks at her parents' before she is off again, although this time she feels, if not excited exactly, then ready. She certainly can't stay here. Emptying the laundry from her travelling holdall, she discards the discoloured underwear and vest tops with pit stains, and removes the rolled-up denim jacket from the bottom of the bag.

She's out, says Kat's younger sister when Eva calls the house phone. She had to look up the number in the big phone book in the kitchen.

Out where?

She's gone jumping, says Claire's bored voice. Out by the Pea Stacks.

Can I have her mobile number, then?

No chance.

Why not? Come on, please.

Nah, I've done that before, never again. If you've not got it, it's because she doesn't want you to have it.

Will she be in later? Can I call back then?

I don't know. She's out jumping most days. You'll have to find her if you want to talk to her.

Eva hates jumping, hates waiting in the dizzying heat at the top of the cliffs before the drop, but she can imagine that Kat enjoys it. Eva is tempted to ask Kat's sister whether jumping off the cliffs into the cold raw sea isn't bad for Kat's heart condition but the shrill beeping has started from where

Claire has already hung up the phone. Eva balls the jacket into a small backpack; she had just assumed that Kat would want it back, although now she's not so sure where such a defined image had come from. She doesn't want to ask her mum for a lift to Jerbourg, aware of all the hateful things that she's said about Kat before, and so she walks to the bus stop that she has used since she was in primary school.

Along the southerly cliff paths, couples are walking their terriers and grandchildren, winding their way through the bracken and wildflowers towards cream teas and weekend newspaper supplements. It is summer as summer should be. The other islands glint gold across the sea like toffee apples. The waves are bright with reflected sunlight, crinkling white and green at the edges. The closer Eva gets to the Pea Stacks, the less the rocks look how Renoir had painted them, the colours of soft fruit and shaded lawns. They are rust-red, angular; a tumble of tired shapes akin to a scrapyard. They put her in mind of shipwrecks.

Eva has been to see the Pea Stacks before, has swum at Moulin Huet and waved at the dog and the lion rocks from afar as a child, but she's never tried to clamber towards the edge of the cliffs. She can hear whoops and shouts from somewhere close to Jerbourg Point. She tries to focus on which ledge to put her foot on next and what tuft of seagrass to hold on to, hauling herself up and across the headland. She is out of breath when she finally spots Kat and her friends at the peak of a bric-a-brac rock structure, her palms and shins scored with pale grazes so that she could never pass it off as no bother.

The boys eye her with curiosity, as if they hadn't gone to school with her for seven years. Eva can feel this new power, and she can tell from the way that Kat looks to the boys and back to Eva that Kat can too. She wants Kat to say something first or rush towards her or make a joke but Kat just squints at her in the sunlight.

Your sister said you'd be here, says Eva.

She speaks, says Kat. Who'd have thought it. So you're back on the rock, then?

Yeah, says Eva. She smiles at the boys in the way that she has learned to. Hi, she adds.

You know Carlos and JC, do you? And this is Tricky.

Nice tan, says Tricky.

They're just going in again, aren't you? Kat tells them.

The boys nod at the girls and, now they realise their conversational contributions are not wanted, they move a little further along the rocks to get a good view of the drop into the deep water below. From up here, some patches of the sea appear so dark that they look solid. The boys continue to linger in earshot, slipping glances back at the girls before looking at the sledging water again.

Pussies, Kat calls over to them. The longer you wait, the worse it gets.

I brought you your jacket back, Eva says. She contorts out of her backpack's straps and reaches inside the drawstring opening for the precious item of clothing that's folded neatly inside. I thought you'd want it.

It's not mine, says Kat before Eva has fully got the denim jacket free of the bag. Kat takes a step back and shakes her head.

You lent it to me, explains Eva with a nod. At the airport. Remember?

I don't think so. I've never seen it. It's not mine.

Well, I got it from you.

It must have been my sister's. Looks like something she'd wear.

I just thought you'd want it back, says Eva, trying to stuff the garment's lagging arms back into her bag.

Any excuse to see me, eh?

The boys all jeer at this. Eva realises that them being curious about her newfound confidence doesn't mean they're on her side. The boys are watching her like a seagull who might nick their chips: they have not decided yet whether to tease or kick. Eva has not felt like this since school, and even then she always felt safe; there were other people who this crowd reliably went for instead. She is aware now of how she used to shrink away, thinking then that she knew how best to protect herself. She decides to smile fully at Kat, steps forward, thinks of the ease with which Kat had spoken to her on the aeroplane. She puts her tongue between her two fingers like Kat had done at the airport and starts to laugh at her boldness.

We're not friends, Kat whispers, slapping Eva's hand away from her mouth. We were never friends.

But on the plane, starts Eva. Eva can hear the ruffling waves from where she is standing but not fully see them, and the effect makes her dizzy. She is holding on to the strap of her backpack as if it were a roof handle in one of the lurching cabs she'd taken in between dive bars in countless towns, clinging on to the worn plastic like it might save her. She looks down at her feet to steady herself and notices that Kat's toenails are carefully painted in alternating shades of purple and mint.

You've come all this way, says Kat loudly, so that all

the boys can hear. Are you not going to go in? You don't fancy a swim?

No, I'm all right, says Eva.

Fair, shrugs Kat. Whatever. She's not going in, she calls back to the boys.

She's not going in? they call back.

Suddenly Kat snatches Eva's hand and runs, dragging her along like a toy cart, the backpack bumping out of her grip, up and over the scrub at the edge of the cliff. Eva is too shocked to protest once she realises what is happening, so she punches her knees up into her chest, her one hand gripping Kat's and the other fastened over her eyes and nose. The water hits her like a bad joke.

Eva is laughing and snorting and yet she hates it. Saltwater scratches the back of her throat and she feels as if she has stubbed all her toes at once. She coughs up seawater and sticking strands of her own hair, gasps with shock and the sharp cold. She kicks her feet in the chilling water, struggling to keep upright against the current, her muscles exhausted. She is so angry that she thrashes out her hand to slap Kat in the face but Kat catches it in hers and closes her fingers over Eva's.

We can't all just fuck off on holiday and leave our lives for a year, Kat says, dragging Eva back towards the base of the rocks.

But I did what you said, Eva protests. You know you said I should go on a banana boat, well I—

What do you want me to say, well done? You did what by yourself, you left? I don't know who you're trying to impress.

Eva thinks she will never be someone who has this kind of power over others, if the secret to being powerful is not to care. But she is learning to pretend. Maybe, she thinks, this is all that Kat is doing herself.

We're not friends, Kat repeats with a howl. Eva can't tell if the rasp in Kat's voice is saltwater or sadness.

Eva scrambles up the rocks behind Kat to hear the boys' laughs. They are roaring at how the seawater dripping down inside Eva's inner thighs looks like piss from fright. Kat passes her a towel without looking at her. Eva dries her face and her arms and legs quickly, the water pooling on the orange granite under her soggy trainers, and retrieves her backpack from where it had landed. She leaves without a word. She can hear the boys' guffaws echoing around the rocks as she scales down to the cliff path. Soon she will dump the denim jacket into the clothes recycling bin along with everything else from the past year that she has spoiled or grown out of.

Eva has two more weeks at home before moving to the mainland. She doesn't go to the South Show, even though her mum enters the gâche contest and comes home with a second-place rosette. Another girl wins Miss Guernsey that year with her speech about saving the whales and her palm-print bikini making the front page in the *Press*. The Vale Earth Fair comes and goes, and Eva cuts out the fraying rainbow braid from her darkening hair. Her tan peels away. The week before Freshers' Week officially starts, Eva takes an early flight to the mainland in the hope that she won't have to sit by anyone she knows on the flight out. She doesn't: she is next to a fifty-something businessman who only speaks to her to ask her to turn her music down. She arrives at Leeds University and finds new friends, boyfriends, girlfriends. She gets more confident in saying no to things as much as saying yes to things.

She won't speak to Kat again apart from on Christmas Eve in 2012 in The Cock and Bull, when Kat is dumb drunk and snide and refusing to engage in Eva's attempts at conversation. Kat's husband tells Eva not to bother and he drinks the pint of water that Eva has got for his wife. Eva will ask Kat if she wants any help for a taxi and Kat will laugh at her, the same old snagging laugh, but far too loud this time. Then Eva won't see Kat again before she dies. But Eva thinks about Kat sometimes, when she takes up swimming confidence lessons for adults in the university pool, coughing up water and smearing chlorine from her eyes so that she can see. And then years later when she is crawling lanes in local leisure centres and the London lidos, and once when she is much older and screaming down a log flume ride in Disneyland with her friend's children, and often at home after a shower, looking in the mirror as she combs her long wet hair straight.

A Kindness

The Rohais, 2004

S he needs a father figure, he thinks.

He rehearses conversation openers in the mirror when he brushes his teeth, checks the weather forecast for the next seven days so he'll have something to say. Sometimes he curates a small selection of guitar-led band CDs to display out on the dashboard for when she first ducks into the car, only to tidy them away when she gets into the seat with a dismissive comment about how the music must be from before she was even born. He thinks of tens of small things that might get her talking, feeling inspired. When the day of the lesson approaches, his excitement is rattling like an egg on the boil.

She's been learning to drive since the day after her seventeenth birthday. It's taken the best part of a year and she hasn't passed her theory test yet and she can't muster the go needed for the island's big roundabout up by the pier. Her clutch control is poor and their lessons are punctuated by stalls, so he's block-booked her for another six lessons. She's not the worst student he's had, though, and the longer she takes, the more he feels confident that he can help her. Helping people is his favourite part of the job.

Their lessons have developed into the following routine. Hi Neil, she'll say, getting in the car up on the corner by the athletics track at her school – call me Neil, he'd insisted on their first lesson, and he was glad that she always did – and they'll drive away from the lunch-hour squabblings and snoggings towards the big supermarket on the Rohais, before getting out and swapping seats. Over the course of the hour, they'll make polite conversation about road theory that will develop into freer discussion as the lesson continues. At the end of every lesson, she asks if he thinks she's any closer to sitting her test, and at the end of every lesson, he says, No, not quite yet, love.

While schooling her in the basics of three- and five-point turns, the importance of mirrors, and the concept of dual carriageways (he shows her a diagram in a driving theory textbook, at this stage in the lesson, as it's not like they can visit the real thing), Neil asks her further questions. Her favourite A level is French and she's got a conditional place at her top choice of university. She's allergic to cats, doesn't like gigs or camping. She doesn't seem to swear, which he thinks is a sign of great maturity at her age. He wants to tell her that it's good to be different. She seems to him a model teenager.

His lessons with other pupils go by like episodes of an afternoon television soap. Seventeen-year-old boys with chubby ties and eye-watering deodorant, pointing out the oversized exhausts on cars as they drive past the Kev Run. Middle-aged mums with lumpy jeans who tell Neil that they've had to learn to drive to the Co-op now that their husbands have left them for secretaries and horse-riding instructors. Older widows who have been tasked with collecting their grandkids from primary school. These people sit in Neil's car all day. They chat a bit, asking how to turn on the windscreen wipers or what happens if you miss your go in a filter-in-turn junction, but they rarely ask a question that isn't about the task in hand.

In between sessions, he likes to drive to the supermarket for a fifty-pence sausage roll and a seventy-four-pence Scotch egg from the deli counter. His GP keeps telling him to cut down on red meat but where's the fun in life, he always jokes. He takes care when it comes to having his daily picnic in the car, rolling down the windows to free the oily smell, collecting the pastry flakes in the plastic bag on his lap. When he's done, he shakes the bag out of the window and runs a wet wipe over his hands and chin. There's a coconut air-freshener tag tied to the rear-view mirror and he gives it a spritz from the refill bottle every fortnight. He wants people to feel comfortable in his space.

He has a drink at The Rockmount most evenings after lessons. Cider first, then a red wine. He likes to get drunk enough that the bungalow doesn't feel quite so quiet when he gets home. He prefers to shit in a toilet that he doesn't have to clean himself. He usually goes for chicken bits and chips with garlic bread on the side, and every now and again he adds breaded garlic mushrooms to the order for a treat. He reads *The Guernsey Press* with his meal, folding it in half so that it sits neatly next to the small pot of ketchup. He diligently keeps up to date with the house prices, football losses, cow thefts, cannabis offences. Sometimes there are some quite beautiful wildlife photography page spreads, shot by local enthusiasts. He likes the puffins.

Today's headline reads CLOSED ROAD NOW OPEN. The bar is full of the usual customers. Kids, mostly, and bottle-nosed alcoholics. There are a couple of scaffolders and fishermen in overalls, who take their pints round to the back bar with its faded felted pool tables, and there is a Frenchman in a windcheater who is asking the barman if the mussels are any good. It's rowdier here in summer, of course, with tourists and toddlers and girls in tie-side bikinis. But tonight it's quiet, and Neil does his best to avoid eye contact with the group of young lads who are slouched beside the quiz machine. He's already read the best bits of the paper but he starts again from the front in an effort to look busy.

One of the lads, a scrub of stubble masking his acne pockmarks, comes over and sits beside him on the bald upholstery. You don't mind, do you, mate, he says.

No, you're perfectly all right there, Neil says.

I guess it's not like you have anyone coming, the lad says. Bit of a loner, eh.

Right, Neil says. He tries to focus on the small classified listing for guinea pigs from a farm in Torteval, which states that they MUST GO this weekend.

The lad pinches a large chip off Neil's plate. Neil makes a jokey tut as if he is letting the boy off. Neil can smell the lager on the lad's breath as he leans over his shoulder to read the advert.

Sounds like a threat, doesn't it? he says, pointing the half-eaten chip at Pets Corner. He rams the remaining chip into Neil's miniature pot of ketchup, scooping up the last transparent smears of red. Sounds like he's going to put the rest of them in the bin, the boy goes on, or in the blender. That's what they do with male chicks, isn't it? They check the sexes of them when they're born and they just chuck the boy chickens into a big mixer.

Neil nods without looking up, staring determinedly at the guinea pigs advert. He pushes another breaded chicken strip into his mouth and chews. The goujon is dry without any ketchup but he can't get out of the seat to fetch another pot, as now the lad's mates are gathering around him too. He has a large swig of Cabernet Sauvignon and stands up.

I need to go to the lavatories, Neil proclaims.

The lad grins, stands up to let Neil go, and picks another chip off his plate with his thumb and forefinger. He eats it with his mouth open, potato pasting his front teeth, as Neil passes and walks to the toilets without looking back. The door swings shut. He unzips his trousers and breathes slowly. As he starts to piss, the door slams open again and the lad enters. He's still chewing on the chip as he looks at Neil.

Do you mind? Neil says.

You're the driving instructor, aren't you, he says. All the girls at school talk about you, you know.

Oh good, Neil says.

About what a pervert you are.

What?

Come on. We've seen you picking them up from school, trying to make them laugh. We know you've got your little favourites.

Favourites?

Josie Chauval, for one. Our mate's little sister. She told us you think she's mature for her age.

Josie Chauval is a good student, he says.

She's seventeen.

Of course she's seventeen, she's learning to drive, he starts to say without any sense of what he's really protesting against.

She says you're always asking her things, asking her what she does on the weekends, who she sees. Why do you want to know stuff like that?

It's called conversation, he says.

Why are you having conversations with seventeen-year-old girls, eh, trying to chat them up? Don't you think that's a bit fucking weird? Do you really think that she wants to spend all her time talking to you?

I don't think that she wants to talk to me, Neil begs.

Glad we've got one thing straight, says the lad.

The others come in then. One of the guys, muggy-eyed and shovel-fisted, asks Neil why he's such a pervert. There's piss on his loafers now, a damp splotch spreading across the weave of his trousers as he tries to jam the zip back up. There's no time to wash his hands. They call him a paedophile first, a drunk-driver second. We see you drinking in the Rocky every night, they say, there's no hiding it. They tell Neil that their cousins are in the police and they'll give them his number plate number if he tries anything.

But I've never touched anyone, Neil says.

So you are a virgin then, the main one laughs. Go on, Paul, you give it to him first.

Someone goes for his face. First the cheekbones, temples, smashing his lips into his teeth. They are all giving it their best then. Neil can feel his ribs go, hot and wet. He doesn't know if he is screaming. He doesn't know how long it is before they give up and leave.

He hopes that nobody will come in and see him, lying under the urinals with his shirt buttons ripped and belly out. But he wishes someone would walk in and help him up. He tries to raise his arm across his chest to cradle his ribs, and pain skewers up along his spine. Muscles, bones, synapses and sinews of all length and breadth: everything hurts. He lies on the reassuring solidness of the tiled floor and considers his options. His coat's still on the bench in the pub, he'll need to collect that. He could call the police, tell them he'd been beaten up in the toilets; but when they ask what the motive could have been, could he really say it's because the local youths have taken to calling him a nonce? He'd lose his customers overnight when the rumour was regurgitated in the *Press*. He's lived alone for years but nobody's ever given him any trouble for it before, and now he wonders how many people have seen him drinking his drinks alone in the pub.

He grabs on to the rim of the sink and hauls himself up. His bloodied reflection is clear enough to see in the mirror. He dabs at his nose and lip with toilet roll, the fluffy fibres sticking at the wounds, and squats under the hand dryer to dry off his trousers. Thick tears are burbling up at the back of his throat. He hasn't been beaten up since school.

The regular drinkers stare at him as he walks out across the carpet and leans, with a whine, to pick up his coat. Someone is sniggering. The flesh around his eyes is puffing up like meat pasties so it's hard to navigate his way out of the swing doors without bumping into the low stools and tables on the way. Someone could easily help him, could wedge an arm under his to steady him, but nobody steps forward. The bar staff all know his name. He wonders if the lads have already spread their filth about him, if all the other regulars are fearful of getting it on their shoes.

He crosses the road and gets into the car. He winds down the windows so that the sea chill slaps his face and takes the taste of cheap wine off his bloodied mouth. The salt in the air stings the cuts and grazes. There are no police on the roads and it's only a short drive home, one that he's made hundreds of times before and in far worse a state than now, but he is struggling to see through the swelling and the tears. He speeds up, desperate to be in bed and out of his seeping clothes. He will have a nightcap at home to try to block out the night. His hands shake when he pours out the whisky.

He wakes in the morning with the sensation that he's slept under concrete. Is this what being buried alive feels like, he wonders, fingering the greying skin over his ribs. The muscles hurt, the joints hurt. The pain bulges as if it's trying to escape from his body. He showers in tepid water but he can't really face a good wash what with the stinging. He steps out, pats himself down with a thin towel, examines his injuries in the mirror. His eyes are inked with bruises, his lips split like figs. The cold sore under his left nostril has opened right up. He is repulsed by his own reflection.

He makes a few phone calls to cancel the day's lessons before heading out to the car. He doesn't normally lock the front door, nobody on his lane ever does, but he worries about the damage that eggs could do to interior paintwork. If the lads from the pub knew his name, then they could easily find out his address. His business cards are tacked up on shop and school noticeboards around the island.

The short walk to the hospital reception desk feels longer than a Saturday supermarket queue. He fills out his details, steadying himself on the desk, and confirms for a second time that no, he doesn't have health insurance and yes, he is self-employed. He doesn't know what MRIs cost but he hopes that he doesn't have to have one.

He sits down in the waiting room, the scratched plastic of the chair rough against his back. The other patients look at him, he looks at them. He's thankful not to recognise any of them through his bloodshot vision.

You'll have your bloods and pressure done by the nurse first, the receptionist says. You'll be called when it's your turn to be seen.

There are bleeps and buzzes and please-hold-stills from behind the closed curtains. Bin lids slam and bundles of laundry are wheeled away by porters. A woman in a white coat is cutting up a birthday cake. It strikes Neil that everyone is involved in a great deal of activity and he's just here to watch. The loneliness hits him like last night's smack in the jaw.

A young male doctor leads him to a cubicle and rakes the curtains across. He sanitises his hands while Neil undresses. He shows him where it hurts, tries not to whimper as he taps his abdomen and ribs.

Tell me again how it happened, the doctor says. His face is smooth and pale like marzipan, his expression one that Neil can't pinpoint.

I don't remember, Neil lies.

Is this the first time you've found yourself in a fight like this, not sure how it started?

I didn't start anything, says Neil.

If it's all right with you, there are a few more tests we'd like to do, including a scan, just to rule out any internal injuries. Do you have insurance?

I'm self-employed, Neil says again.

He leaves the hospital with a prescription for codeine and a follow-up appointment with a gastroenterologist. He arranges a large bulldog clip over his seat belt to stop it from tugging at his torso too tightly. It'll take a few weeks to pay off the hospital bill. He measures the various pains of his body on the drive home, wondering whether tomorrow will be too soon to get back to lessons. He winces with the effort it takes to let off the handbrake.

His clients say that they don't understand his need to reschedule and Mrs De Garis isn't the only individual to threaten to move to another instructor. Neil crosses out the appointed times in his diary, moving them a week or two ahead. Flipping through the pages, he sees that the only upcoming appointments he has are driving lessons and now one with the consultant. No holidays, no birthdays, Sunday lunches or get-togethers. He does have family on the island but Christmases there are about carving up the farmland in the wills. The diary is full only of empty weekdays and weekends. Apart from the next lesson with Josie, underlined three times and scheduled for Wednesday at three fifty after school. He doesn't want to cancel on her, thinking that she must enjoy the regular company and grown-up conversation. He remembers then how they had spat at him when he was writhing on the floor of the Gents, and he hopes that the lads don't see him picking her up. He wonders which of them was her brother, if he had really been there at all.

The engine tuts as he waits at the bottom of the school car park for Josie, as far away from the school gates and bus bays as he can get. He stretches his palm across the worst of his face, masking the sight from any passing students. It's the end of the school day, the kids are whooping towards the bus stops, pushing each other over the pavement and ripping open bags of crisps. Neil watches the rear-view mirror for signs of Josie. He spies a boy being piled on by a group of sixth-formers, his textbooks splayed across the tarmac. Neil is watching the scene so intently that it makes him jump when Josie opens the boot and slings her backpack inside.

Are you okay? she asks. He reaches up to run his fingers through his hair, trying to hide the discoloured mess of his face. He avoids her gaze as he gets out of the car and slopes around to the passenger door.

You can drive from here for a change, he says as he eases himself gently into the seat, careful to wedge his hand under the seat belt so that it doesn't tug at his sore chest. Out of the pillowy corner of his right eye, he can see that she is frowning. She peers at him, not starting the ignition.

Are you sure you're okay?

Oh come on, just because you don't want to do the round-about today, he jokes. We'll go up to La Vrangue first so you can warm up. You can try some reverse parking in the Post Office depot. Then we'll go through Vauvert and the back of town towards St Martin's to give you a bit of practice with the traffic lights and hill starts. Does that sound good to you?

Okay, she says without nodding, and readjusts her seat. She starts up the engine.

Neil places his feet over the secondary pedals just in case, the pain bolting up from his hamstrings to his shoulders. He smiles encouragingly at her and she veers very, very slowly out of the school car park and into the main road.

The lesson continues much like it always does, although he

lets her do more of the talking. He learns, as Josie attempts to reverse-park the car between the two white lines, that she has achieved an A in her English Literature coursework. She tells him that she will spend the weekend revising for her exams and then hanging out with some of her friends. He is feeling nauseated from the painkillers so he winds the windows down wide, the fresh air stinging slightly at the cuts and grazes on his cheeks.

As Josie drives them down La Route Des Camps at an appropriate speed, Neil's phone rings. His bruised ribs twinge as he reaches into his jacket pocket for his mobile. He looks at the screen and doesn't recognise the number. He rarely receives phone calls from people who aren't his clients, and he has diligently saved all of their details on his SIM.

I'll leave it, he says out loud, worried that the lads from The Rockmount have found his driving school advert in the phone book or on the supermarket pinboard and have decided to torment him. The phone continues to ring. As soon as it stops, it starts again.

You can get it, I don't mind, Josie says, failing to judge the narrow width of the road and bumping the tyre on the pavement. Before he asks her to pull over, Neil reminds Josie never to answer the phone while driving, and adds that now you could get done for eating a KitKat while in charge of the wheel too. They stop in the close behind St Martin's Garage and Neil nods at her to put on the handbrake. With difficulty, Neil hauls himself out of the car and shuts the door.

Who is this? Neil says quietly into the handset, conscious that Josie is in the nearby car and sitting with the window open. He looks at her and she quickly looks out of the window at the petrol pumps.

It's Dr Le Conte, the doctor says. He explains that he has spoken to one of his colleagues about the results of the MRI scan. We were looking for any internal damage from your recent injuries, any internal bruising of organs and soft tissues, he says, but there was something else the radiologist noted that we have been concerned about and since properly discussed. Is now a good time to talk?

At the end of the conversation, in which Neil has been invited back to the Princess Elizabeth for a contrast medium scan and a laparoscopy to observe the size and spread of the tumour, he's asked if he has someone he can talk to. Neil says no, he does not, and they say that when he next comes into the hospital, the consultant will issue him with a referral for the local cancer counselling service. Once they've agreed on a treatment plan, they'll also have him talk to the specialist nurse about ways to improve his lifestyle, his diet, his drinking. Neil thanks the doctor for his call and pushes the red button on his mobile handset. He takes a moment before folding himself back up and into the car.

Josie has switched the engine off. Her eyes are wetting at their cat's-eye corners. She's managed to pull the handbrake up fully and park in parallel to the next vehicle. Neil coughs.

Come on, let's carry on, he says, looking around as if to check that there aren't any other cars reversing but really because he's worried about being unable to hide the fear in his face. He imagines the greying sprigs of hair on his head being shaved off while he watches afternoon television, a tea towel draped around his shoulders; his stomach peeling away from his body and the skin on the back of his hand as thin as clingfilm around the cannula. His throat is in a stranglehold and he reaches towards his gut as if he can feel it.

Are you all right? Josie says. She's crying, shiny tears pearling the soft down of her cheeks and upper lip.

I walked into a door, Neil says, waving away his bruises with one hand. He winces at the pain in his shoulder. Silly old me.

I didn't mean to listen, I couldn't help it. My dad had bladder cancer in January. It was horrible. He had to have surgery, I found out just before my last theory test. My brother Paul said to give it a go anyway, it might be good for me, but I think that's why I failed, I've been finding it really hard to concentrate lately.

Really, he says.

Yeah, she says. I'm really sorry.

He tries to tell her that she doesn't need to be sorry for anything but he's finding his throat too thick and tight. Josie reaches over towards him, the seat belt straining to hold her back, and she puts her arms around his neck. Neil scans the garage forecourt for signs of anyone watching. Josie continues to hug him. Neil eventually puts his arms around her too.

He holds her tightly and closes his eyes.

Liberation Day

St Peter Port, 2011

Being such a good-looking man on a small island was not without its challenges. Goody had worked his way through most of the women on Guernsey; the only ones left were too ugly or housebound or good little wives, his mates would rib him. Them and his pupils, whose fierce crushes he was relieved not to return. It would take a public celebration of impolite scale to smoke out any remaining females hitherto untouched by his hands, and Goody was ready to find them. The Liberation Day fair couldn't come soon enough.

The fair on the Albert Pier car park started setting up three days before the big event. The workers had been at the West Show the previous week, cramming the waltzers with children while their parents watched cattle shows and got battered in the cider tents. These peripatetic parish shows were just a warm-up for the main event on the ninth of May, everyone knew: it was a chance to acclimatise the liver, sport your first sunburn of the year, make a public pass at your chosen sexual partner to ensure that nobody else would. There were no maypoles these days but alcohol and mating and male pride remained at the heart of the island's festivities. Goody had three days to decide which woman he wanted to parade around with.

Goody had the kind of body women liked to be under. He knew that because they were, regularly, noisily. They buckled into his hands on street corners and car seats and holiday cottage beds. They came when he instructed them to. He was tall, which distinguished him enough in pubs and nightclubs that he rarely had to fabricate an opening line of conversation. Being a teacher brought with it an assumed disposition of sensitivity and kindness, the expectation of which Goody never fulfilled: he never called his bedfellows back or stopped to chat when he'd inevitably see them in the Pollet. Some of his pass-offs he would see at parents' evening, queueing up to talk about their children while crossing and recrossing their legs under the diminutive tables. Women would wonder what they had done wrong and Goody would wonder when he'd meet someone worth a second date. He was disappointed when his flings told him how they felt, finding it unfair that so many people could develop such an intense sense of affection so quickly when he couldn't. The bitter fallout from his one-nighters was beginning to bore him more than the routine of the dates themselves.

So when he met Eva again after all this time, his erection felt like a prophecy. Eva had blonde hair, eyes the bright blue of swimming-pool covers, and a German grandfather who was said to have worked in the Alderney camps during the war. Goody still remembered her primary school show-and-tell presentation, talking through the PVA-glued branches of her family tree with a look of almost painful concentration. They had gone to secondary school together as well as primary, but there wasn't much in particular he remembered about her from that later time. She'd avoided the bus parties, had declined hook-ups and spins in cars. Then she had left the island for university and not returned, not even for Christmas, or certainly not any time he'd ever seen her, until this summer when Goody happened upon her outside the Beau Séjour leisure centre.

Goody preferred to go to the gym for a quick workout before the school day started. It was early, the light was blotched and watery. He saw her across the car park and called out, and she turned around sharply as if he was trying to steal something. She didn't hug him, though she did smile, and then proceeded to unlock her car boot while he spoke. She had been for a swim, her wet hair heavy on her untanned shoulders, and he thought that she must have forgotten to bring a bra because he spied her nipples blackberrying through her T-shirt. He said he hadn't seen her in going on ten years and would she like to come out to the De La Rue for a pint?

I'm not planning on being back on the rock for very long, she said.

Long enough for a drink, though, he said.

I'm not really drinking right now, she said, twisting out fat chlorinated droplets from her ponytail. And anyway, she added, even if I was, I'm broke.

How about this then? he said. You can fuck me for free.

She rolled her eyes and he laughed at the openness of her indignation. At school, her reserve had struck him as stuck-up; now, compared to his typical interactions with women, it seemed novel. You could tell she'd lived on the mainland, he thought, the distance had crept into her voice. Middle-aged women with their swimsuits swinging in carrier bags turned to look at the two of them talking. Goody wondered if the onlookers thought they were already a couple.

You know you want to, Goody persevered, a line that normally had women pushing aside underwires and rumpling up their dresses.

But instead Eva was closing the car boot, opening the driver's door, leaning on the seat as she swapped her flip-flops for trainers without bothering to put socks on. He noted that she was not looking in his direction.

That much of a rush, eh? he said as if he was in on the joke.
Sorry?

What? He lowered his voice. Honestly, it'd be good to hang out. If you're only back for a few days, maybe we could hang out tomorrow? Catch up?

She made a small noise while she tied her shoelaces. She straightened her long skirt and said, Sorry but I promised I'd babysit my little cousin tomorrow. I don't get to see him very often so I can't let him down. We're going to go to Herm for the day.

I'm great with kids, Goody said.

Good for you, Eva laughed and tucked her flip-flops into a tote bag. She got into the driver's seat.

It's true, he added. I'm a teacher. I'm even first aid trained. If you fell in, I could rescue you.

If I fell in what? The sea?

Yeah.

So you're a lifeguard now too.

I can do mouth-to-mouth.

Right, she said, her hand on the handbrake. She put her sunglasses on and he couldn't see where her eyes went.

Seriously, though. I would love to come.

With me and my little cousin, really?

Weather's meant to be good. Nice day for Herm. So it's a date?

You don't take no for an answer, do you?

So I can get your number?

I can't remember my Guernsey number, I don't use it enough.

Your mainland one, then.

She paused, tilting her head to one side in a way that Goody felt was coy. We're getting the first boat over. If you're able to get to the clock tower for eight then I guess we'll see you there. It's not a date, though.

Sure, he said. It's not a date.

Goody went on inside to the gym, groin thrumming with achievement. He did the cross trainer, the rowing machine. He ran fifteen kilometres while watching oiled dancers shimmying to drum and bass on the subtitled television in the corner. He thought how impressive he would look with his top off on Shell Beach tomorrow. He would play volleyball with Eva's little cousin, buy them all ice creams, and slick suncream all over Eva's pale back. Then he would take her to a cool cave for a hot fuck.

The remaining day at school dragged its heels, the students asking Goody questions about photosynthesis that he couldn't be bothered to explain. In the all-staff meeting, his colleagues were complaining about the need for more than one microwave. Goody nodded along, stirring fruit-flavoured protein powder into his milk, and tried to imagine what Eva would have done with her pubic hair. He then spent his last lesson teaching Year 8 the rudiments of respiration, trying to remember his last shag. He couldn't picture her face; could only remember the hipster-kitsch flower print that was hung on the wall above her bedstead. He had known that he didn't really fancy her beforehand but he went along with it anyway. Waking up in her bed the next morning had filled him with a kind of despondence. He had since had the idea that he'd better have a wank before future dates, to prevent himself from getting carried away and ending up in the same dismal situation again. Not that this was a concern with Eva, though, he was sure.

He had two pints at the pub with the lads before he went home to mark homework. Burping down his cider, Jamie said that Goody was going to ruin his average, taking his time with a girl like that; Marc, whose engagement was overshadowing the summer, said it was about time Goody settled on someone. The Queripel brothers said they couldn't remember Eva from school but suggested that Goody should bring her to town on Liberation Day so they could get a good look at her.

They had all been on Brian's stag do the year before, a Friday-to-Sunday Jersey affair where they'd found a local brothel stabling European forty-somethings. Goody, eager to get the night going and lead the party, took his pick, without realising that there weren't bedrooms to take the women to. He couldn't bottle it. So he'd done it there with the woman on the plush sofa, surrounded by the others, eyes sliding over the lino floor and the bruised thighs churning up and down around his back. It wasn't how they thought it would be, but the others had a go too. They paid in twenties and took Brian to the zoo the next day to look at the lemurs. Brian got married the week after and they never spoke of the night after that. In fact, they barely spoke of Brian's wedding again, rarely asked about his wife.

Goody regretted mentioning Eva and loudly turned the pub talk towards football scores, sand racing and boxsets. One more pint down and he walked the dark lanes home.

Gulls were picking at last night's kebabs on the pier. Crates were being stacked on the milk boat, the new day's newspapers damp from the spray. French tourists were thwacking their sandalled feet across the decks of their yachts, drinking cups of coffee as they watched the buoys and empty plastic bottles bob about on the water. Goody bought three day-return tickets for the Herm Travel Trident, biting his lip at the cost. It'll be worth doing properly, he thought, handing over the cash. He would appear mature, thoughtful. A steady bet. She'd lap it up.

He was wearing his failsafe black T-shirt that showed off his tattooed biceps and disguised the flourishing patches of nervous sweat. He was never usually nervous. He nipped off to do a line of coke in the public loos and re-emerged to the vision of Eva in a sundress and broad-brimmed hat, like a seaside postcard from somewhere he wouldn't have bothered visiting before. She hadn't worn make-up and he could see freckles peppering her cheeks and forehead. She stepped towards him and beckoned to her younger cousin to follow.

Although this wasn't what he would call a little cousin, Goody thought resentfully. This was Luc Batiste, the scourge of Year 10. He had boots for fists and dealt spice in the lay-by during lunch breaks. Teachers routinely exemplified Luc as someone who would do nothing with his life if he carried on like that; more than one teacher had called Luc a waste of everyone's time. Only last week, Goody had given the kid detention for putting his hand up a sheep's lung in the laboratory and puppeteering it in the face of another pupil, who had to go home to his mother with piss-soaked trousers. Goody had struggled to explain to the headteacher how it had happened. Most of the boys at the school respected Goody, envying his easy manner and strength. Sometimes Goody swam lengths in the school pool to purposefully show off his powerful masculine frame to the viewing gallery above.

Luc says that you two know each other, said Eva.

Goody nodded. Was this a test, he wondered. Was she testing his determination, the strength of his attraction, by bringing along this boy who she surely knew was a hoodlum? Luc was one of the few kids who never failed to disrupt his lessons, smoke openly on the steps, or cram peers' heads into the concrete paving stones outside the cafeteria. Eyeing up his science teacher now, Luc spat through the gap in his front teeth onto the ground. He didn't smile and kept his eyes fixed on the soft spot just below Goody's ribs. Luc would tell everyone at the school about this, Goody knew, so the date had better be a success.

All right, sir, Luc said.

Lovely day for it, Goody challenged.

The small inter-island ferry coughed up alongside the pier and Goody offered his hand to help Eva step on board. She took it with a wrinkle of her lip and proceeded to the top deck, where Luc sat a few seats behind them and lit up a Marlboro Light. Eva held her hat against the wind and her nose against the diesel ferry fumes. Goody asked her about herself in the hope that she would offer him an opportunity to flirt. He said he wanted to know what happened to her after they'd finished school. She complied with a slight nod, as if she'd been tasked to do something at work.

She had gone travelling before university, backpacked her way around South America, saw turtles hatching and cycled mountain paths and made friends in bars. It wasn't that original really, she said, it was a lot of sitting around and drinking and taking photos. She was lucky to go, though, she admitted; she would recommend the experience to any eighteen-year-old.

Getting drunk, laughed Goody.

Not just that, she said. Anyway, I try not to drink too much any more.

I'll get you drunk, eh, he said. He shifted in his seat as she squinted, whether at him or the direct sunlight on the water behind him, he couldn't quite tell.

Do you always feel you have to say things like that? she said.

Goody liked her so much that he began acting professionally around her: clasping his hands in his lap as if he was in a job interview and saying please, thank you, would you mind if I. He had never been asked so many questions about himself. Why had he gone back to teach in their old school, did it feel strange? Why did he have a bull inked on his arm, was he a Taurus and did he believe in horoscopes? How had he felt when his father died? Women tended to go straight for his mouth but Eva didn't seem to notice when he brushed her milky thigh with his fingers or breathed on her neck. She was more engaged in pointing out the seabirds on the rocks near Jethou, and explaining how, as a teenager, she'd found the sea more like a fence than a field and had to move to the mainland to stop hyperventilating every time she saw it. She'd lived in Leeds, Manchester, London. Places Goody had only seen on the news. He didn't admit to her that he was afraid of driving on dual carriageways because it was something he'd never done. She'd taken the Tube, been to photography exhibitions, eaten at Korean barbecues: she had done things that made his home feel cast off in the sea further than he'd ever thought. He started to feel seasick and tried to focus on the horizon. He wanted to hold her hand.

Herm approached across the water with its humpback and quaint harbour. Luc didn't say a word to Goody as the trio picked their way across the seaweed-silked rocks, but Eva made polite conversation when the silences soaked in. She wasn't coy, sarcastic or pliant. She was amused at the baskets of urchins and seashell wind-chimes strung up outside Herm's one gift shop. Inside, she bought a stick of rock and a flat coiled shell the colour of rhubarb. Goody tried to make a joke but couldn't come up with something quick enough, his chest tightening up in unfamiliar panic. So instead he bought her a starfish fridge magnet. Luc waited for them outside, another cigarette smouldering on his bottom lip. Tourist paraphernalia in hand, Goody and Eva traipsed uphill through the humid hedgerows and stone-splintered paths towards the beach. Goody was sure he could hear Luc sniggering behind them, although maybe it was the guillemots and shags on the headland.

His trainer socks had slipped down and his heels were blistering. For an island only a mile long, Herm was hard to traverse. Conversation was difficult to follow as they hiked in single file up and down the ragged walkways. Eva led the way without stopping, certain in her directions. Already the sun overhead was hot, coppering their necks. Their shoulders sagged under backpacks. Goody painfully needed a piss but felt he'd sound as young as Luc if he asked to stop, so decided he'd wait till they went for a swim.

They rounded the headland and the beach flashed white through the ferns. Shell Beach was one long stretch of sponge-baked sand, parched and bleached and overexposed. Wet-suited children collected unremarkable shells in buckets and thrashed about in the turquoise sea. Not a cool cave in sight. Only a kiosk, selling luxury clotted-cream ice cream and microwaved pies. At least, Goody thought, they wouldn't be bothered further by Luc, who had already stripped off his top to reveal alarmingly burly arms and declared he would swim out to the boats and back. He was an especially strong swimmer, Eva explained, because he bought drugs off a Normandy fisherman and regularly swam out to meet the boat. Don't look so surprised, Eva said at Goody's frown, you can't be that naïve? Surely there are no real secrets at your school?

I'm still his teacher.

You were the one who was so keen to come along.

Goody took this as his cue to kiss her.

What are you doing? she said into his lips. She got her book out then and shifted onto her front to read.

He took his T-shirt off. He rolled onto his back and hoiked himself up onto his elbows, sunning his body. Rather than untying the knots on her bikini top in response, Eva continued to read. After a time, floundering for a conversation topic that he could confidently own, he asked her if she had any tattoos.

Not me, she said.

You didn't get any when you were travelling? he persisted.

She said no, and politely asked about the overlapping patterns on Goody's body. He was going to get an anchor next, as anchors are symbols of hope and today he was feeling particularly hopeful.

Well, you should get one if you want to, she said. Why not?

Really? he said.

She re-opened her book. Goody hadn't thought to bring a book – didn't have them in the house if he was honest, other than the textbooks he used to teach from – but he twisted onto his front with the sun on his back so that his face was close to hers. He noticed how the light picked up the fair hairs across her forearms. Her breathing was steady and she turned the pages at regular intervals: she did indeed seem to be really reading. Goody made occasional huffs but she didn't engage. She didn't look up again until Luc surfaced from the cold sea, sprinkling seawater and asking for a cheeseburger.

Do you want chips too? Eva said.

Let me get them, Goody said, not wanting to be left alone with Luc.

A cheeseburger, Luc said. A double. Don't forget the ketchup.

Say please, said Eva.

Please, sir.

You don't have to call me sir.

Why's he here again?

Luc.

Goody wanted to ask Luc why he was such a little twat, why Eva had brought him along at all, but he calmly nodded and padded off in the direction of the kiosk further up the dunes. He wondered whether Eva genuinely liked Luc. Maybe she liked kids as a general concept, he thought, as he squidged watery ketchup onto the burger patties. Maybe she wanted a family. Maybe he wanted a family too, he thought, returning to the cousins with the stack of napkin-wrapped burgers in his hand.

Luc took his burger without a thank-you and dropped his latest fag-end into Goody's can of Fanta. Goody sensed Eva watching his reaction so he said nothing, eating his own thin gritty burger with a forced smile, chewing through the hard unknowable bits, and restrained himself from barking at the boy in his customary teacher's voice.

Tastes like shit, Luc said after a while.

You eat that, do you? Goody said.

He saw Eva wince ever so slightly, and Luc smiled. Goody felt further annoyed when Luc asked Eva for the end of her Coke, but refrained from making any comment. When Luc asked Eva to reapply the low-factor suncream on his back, sitting in front of her so that he was facing Goody, he mouthed the words FUCK YOU. Goody could say nothing, being in full view of Eva. Luc did something disgusting with his tongue and then spat on the sand not far from Goody.

Don't do that, love, Eva said, with a surety that Goody took courage from. I bet you don't behave like that in front of Rob in school, do you?

Luc looked at Goody with a raised eyebrow. He made a slight motion with his left hand, a gesture that Goody was always telling the kids off for making.

No, Goody replied.

You're all done, Eva said.

Thanks, Luc said. He trundled back to the shoreline, his back sheening.

I might have a dip too, Eva said, arching up. Would you mind staying here and watching our things?

It'll be colder in there than it looks.

That's kind of the point, she said, nudging him with her heel.

Goody watched her wade out into the water with the sense that he was losing control of the situation. The two heads jounced over the waves towards the horizon. At least, he thought, they couldn't be talking about him when they were swimming so steadily. He looked at Eva's handbag and resented having to babysit it.

As the evening crept in with the tide, they ambled over to the village and the view of La Manche and its scraggy islands unfolded around them. Channel ferries and fishing boats and luxury yachts glinted past the horizon on their way to the Mermaid Tavern for barbecued scallops and cider. Goody offered to go to the bar to buy the drinks and Luc followed, telling Eva that he would help carry them back.

Buy me a pint, Luc said at the bar.

I don't think so, Goody said.

No?

No.

She won't go for you, you know. You're not her type.

Oh really? Because what do you know about adults?

That they're just like kids, Luc said.

Two pints of Rocquette's, please, Goody ordered.

You know that the lads in school only listen to you because you're the teacher. It's not because they respect you, Luc said.

I could think of a lot of things to tell them after this that'd make them respect you even less.

Goody turned to Luc. What do you want?

A pint of cider and black, yeah?

And a cider and black, Goody said to the barman. He carried away his and Eva's glasses, leaving Luc to retrieve his. The more Luc drank, the more he withdrew from conversation, and the quicker Goody stood up to buy the next round. Luc drank himself sick on four pints and while he was in the toilets throwing up, Goody leaned over and pushed his tongue into Eva's mouth. She laughed and then gave in. He put his hand on her chin and felt her jaw shift with a smile. She tasted of salt and Tabasco. On the last ferry home, swaying with alcohol and sunstroke and the shimmying waves, he put his arms around her and kissed her again.

He texted her when he got home to say what a nice day he'd had, too tipsy from the cider and the heat to notice until after he'd pressed send that Herm had autocorrected itself to Hell. He followed up by asking if she wanted to come to the fair with him on Liberation Day. He had a shower in the time it took her to reply but she did say yes, okay, she could come for a bit early on. He went to sleep with one arm around a pillow and woke up in the morning with a hangover, his heart racing like a greyhound. He knew what he would do.

The old quarter of St Peter Port was mottled with cobbled streets and granite. Smears of cleaning fluid clouded the shop windows. There were pubs that only the fishermen frequented, antique shops that were empty except for on the weekends. The streets took a sharp upward turn as the land climbed towards St Martin's; you could take a good look at the harbour from here, not that many tourists ventured this far. They didn't put this part of town on the postcards. Goody's footsteps echoed on the stone passageways as he strode to see the only man willing to risk trade on a Sunday.

The tattoo parlour was run by Pierre, whose arms were lathered with frigates and mermaids and skulls retching up snakes. Pierre had learned his trade in St Malo and had come to Guernsey when the promise of agriculture was still good, but there hadn't been much money to make from tomatoes even then. Instead he had turned a steady hand to pin-dipped artistry.

There was a quietness between the men in Pierre's shop, one grimacing with concentration and the other with pain. Goody had come to Pierre over the years for an assortment of inkings: a compass, the stampeding bull Eva had liked so much, a string of gulls under his left nipple, an octopus across his back. The octopus Goody regretted, its suckers sagging across his shoulders when he didn't do enough weights at the gym. However, he didn't regret that one so much as the name DAVE tattooed on his left buttock by Dave, who'd said it would be a laugh, when it certainly hadn't been at the time and didn't feel like it fifteen years on. Dave didn't even come to the pub any more now that he had kids, so sometimes it felt to Goody that the tattoo was their only connection. Pierre had offered to correct the design and cover it with something else but Goody had refused.

What do you want today? Pierre asked, palms gesturing at the transfer options.

I was thinking about an anchor, Goody replied.

Pierre nodded, his eyes roaming over Goody's body. Could do, he said. Where?

There's a gap on my wrist still, Goody went on, revealing the creamy underside and circling an area of skin that was plump with veins.

And why'd you be wanting it? Pierre asked. He'd known Goody long enough to know he rarely had a reason, but Goody had phoned only yesterday for an urgent appointment, and there was a warble in his voice that Pierre worried would result in a redone job soon enough.

My grandfather was a sailor, Goody replied. It wasn't a lie as such, his grandfather had fished in the Channel for a good forty years of his sixty-seven. But he knew he wasn't adorning his body for the sake of a grandfather whom he'd only met twice, deaf and shouting at the plastic shot glasses of pills handed to him by his carer.

So you can lie to men as well as women now?

I met a girl, Goody said eventually.

I also met a girl once, mused Pierre. I did her a keyhole on her ribs, just below her heart. She had a laugh like the sea and tits made for children. She moved to Marseille, I think, or Berlin. She asked me never to draw the key that would fit her design on any man. She was like that.

Like what? Goody asked.

Hurt, Pierre said.

Oh, Goody said.

Pierre snapped on a pair of disposable gloves. Goody offered his forearm and Pierre set to work. It burnt like a lit match. He distracted himself by picturing the surprised smile he would see on Eva's face when she saw it. Once it was done, Pierre threw the overstretched gloves in the bin like used condoms. He wiped off the excess ink and blood, admired his fine-lined work and explained that he wouldn't be going to the Liberation Day fair tomorrow. He didn't like the fights, he said, or the food.

The fair's good for a laugh, though, eh, Goody said.

You don't always have to laugh. You wouldn't want me laughing with the needle in my hand.

Goody waved his way down the street towards home, where he changed his bedsheets and wiped the hairs from the shower tiles. He couldn't face the tiny squares of the exercise books piled up on his kitchen counter. He threw the uneaten third of his stir-fry in the bin and did thirty pull-ups on the bar outside his bedroom door. He moisturised his tattoos and carefully propped his newly etched wrist up on a pillow. With the lights off and the moon jeering through the shutters, he thought about Eva on his mouth. The night widened like a desert as he waited.

Goody couldn't remember when he had last invited a girl to the fair. Sure, he'd picked them up from fried fish stands and drinks tents and gigs in bars, had had his hands around and inside them at fried fish stands and drinks tents and bars, but a planned invitation was entirely new. He was wearing a new shirt with shoes shiny as a Labrador's nose. He'd resisted the urge to have a tinny at home and rejected the boys' offer of a pint in the Admiral on the walk down through town. The boys would be on their third now, or fourth, the bubbles swilling nicely in anticipation of burgers and dodgems. Goody felt heady with sobriety.

With his wrist wrapped in clingfilm and smeared with antiseptic, Goody waited by the monument on the Albert Pier. The fair was banging now, sausages undercooking and candyfloss churning to the tune of screaming teenagers and throbbing pop. Fluorescent lights flashed and the gravity wheel span and the wait felt extraordinarily long. When Eva did walk up towards him, she turned so that he could kiss her on the cheek rather than the mouth, and kept her hands tucked away in her skirt pockets.

Look, he said, presenting his tattoo. It smiled underneath the sheen of ointment. Admittedly it would take a few days before it was really presentable; however, its blue outline and curling ropes wound proudly across his skin. The bloodied dots around its circumference made it all the more impressive, he felt, for showing the pain behind the pattern.

Eva traced her fingers around the edge of the wrap.

What do you reckon? he breathed.

Looks cool.

Cool, he said.

I looked up what you said about hope when I got home and couldn't find any truth in it, she said. All I could find about anchors was Christian symbolism and I didn't think you were religious, are you? Obviously it's fine if you are.

She challenged him on a lot of things the way most girls wouldn't, or hadn't. He had always assumed that women didn't ask him serious questions because they were waiting for him to ask them to bed. Now he wondered whether they didn't talk to him like that because they thought he didn't have anything interesting to say. He was out of practice.

My grandfather was a sailor, he said quickly.

Ah right, she said. Her eyes veered over towards the fair.

Do you want to go on a ride?

It'll be full of kids at this time, she said. She must have seen the crash in his countenance because then she touched his arm and said, How about we go for a walk first? See what else is on?

St Peter Port's three piers were jostling with families and drunken teenagers. There were ice-cream blobs on the tarmac and plastic cups nodding in the harbour. The only way to move through the crowds was to walk in single file, so they kept their elbows out and didn't speak to one another.

At intervals they stopped: for a can of ginger beer, for a cider, for a polystyrene tray of grilled seafood. Goody wasn't sure exactly what they were walking towards but he was struggling to come up with an alternative. He hadn't thought further than getting her somewhere quiet, and now he wasn't sure where that could be. They forked out shrivelled cockles from their shells, watched a milk float of junior mermaids glide past Marks & Spencer, their green and teal sequins gleaming in the sun. Eva answered his questions just as she had done before, but Goody felt his words running out before he'd even said them.

We could go to the lighthouse, he said.

I thought you wanted to be in town, she said. You won't get much of the party all the way up there.

We could get a good spot for the fireworks. There's always a good view up by the castle.

I probably won't be staying that late, she said. I did say I'd only come for a bit. I'm only back to see my mum for a few days.

It's not Liberation Day without the fireworks, said Goody.

It's the same day whatever you do, she said. Comes around once a year on the ninth.

You make it sound like something to tick off your list.

Maybe I'm just not as fussed about it, not living here.

But you're from here.

How about we go to the fair? You wanted to earlier.

Maybe I could win you a toy, he said.

I bet you say that to all the girls.

She knew about him, he thought then. Him and his women. A week ago he would have been proud to have every islander know about his multitudinous conquests, to have it printed in the *Press* and pinned on the noticeboards in Candie Cache. Now he could see how Eva shrank from their association.

I'm not like that, he said as they struggled through the crowds towards the fair. He wasn't sure whether she'd heard over the noise but he didn't want to risk sounding stupid by repeating it. He was also wary of using charm now: the more successful his tricks, the more she would doubt his honesty. So he said simply, You're not like that to me. You're like catnip.

I prefer dogs to cats, she said, as they crammed into the acid-lit wonderland on the pier.

Bodies shifted through the din in front of them, streaming towards the stalls and the rides and the portable toilets. They squeezed past people he worked with, people he'd been to school with, people he'd taught who now had jobs and flats and girlfriends of their own. They smiled at him so broadly that he felt his shaken confidence recover at the attention. Here he was, at a fair, with a woman of his choosing, for the whole island to see. A woman, not a girl: the real deal. Goody looked back at the crowds and turned to look at Eva.

She lightly touched her hand on his then and it fed his crush like a fever. He leaned in towards her but she jolted away, angled her face back from his, her shoulders up like windbreaks. He straightened his stoop, resisting the urge to shrug. She parted her lips to speak but held the words back. It must be important, he thought, the time she was taking with it. There was a pause in which his hearing throbbed with panic and he tried not to blink so much. He looked away and focused on the rows of lurid green and pink toy mice and elephants in front of them. He read and reread THREE SHOTS FOR A FIVER and CORRECT CHANGE WELCOME.

I don't feel romantically about you, she said. I'm really sorry.

It's all right. I don't care, he said.

I'm just not looking for anything like that at the moment.

I really don't care, he said. He kept his gaze fixed on the soft toy animals.

Right. What are you going to do now, are you going to go and see your friends? Get a drink in time for the fireworks?

Why bother, he thought. And to her he said, Sound, yeah. No worries. I was going to meet up with them later anyway.

I'll see you around then.

Aren't you going back to the mainland soon?

I am, yeah, she said. Soon.

She kissed him on the cheek and pushed off through the crowds. She didn't look back. He stood, sensing his own prominent height. He placed his fist on the stall in front to steady himself. Then he put a five-pound note on the table and took up the toy pistol, popping blindly at the stuck-down tin cans on the shelf. No luck. He thanked the vendor and moved on to the next stall, where he shot one of the metal birds off its perch and still lost two pounds fifty. He bought a cone of marshmallows with the third stall's change but the icing sugar and coloured cornflour made him feel sick and stuck to his throat, so he handed them to a teenage couple lazing by the ghost train.

She did not feel romantically about him, she had said. Or had she said something else too? There must have been other reasons she had hinted at during the day, quiet comments of distrust or disagreement. There must have been. But already he could feel what was said and not said disintegrating at the edges like a sandcastle. She had said a lot that day on Herm too, her tits glazed with suncream and bikini ties tugging at her hips, and yet he couldn't remember any of it. Perhaps he hadn't been listening. Perhaps he hadn't been listening for a long time.

He didn't answer his mates' calls when they rang nor did he bother to return them, and instead toured the remainder of the fair by himself. He played the ducks, the frogs, hit the anvil like a strongman. He went home without a prize and with the new anchor tattoo in navy ink dragging him under. The lanes were empty and rustling with May's pink blossom as he walked away from the town. When they came, the fireworks overhead shot the night sky to pieces.

Mein Herr

L'Ancresse, 2012

September has settled with a smart wind and a rattle in the stripping trees, and the season's colours are beginning to stipple the headland. L'Ancresse Common is booby-trapped with rabbit holes so the students are running slowly, delicately stepping around the slippery stains of alpine moss. The teachers are huddled in one of the only sheltered patches of land behind an outcrop of rocks. The female teaching staff are flirting with the ambulance men, waiting it out until one of the students breaks an ankle or sprains a knee. Mascara is smeared like tears over the faces of the sixth-form girls as they huff their way across the makeshift cross-country course.

You can do it, Mr Martel shouts at his students. A flurry of middle fingers stick up at him as the students bob past but he does not let his encouraging smile falter.

Headmaster, comes a strained voice in his direction. Mr Priaulx lumbers over the headland like a woodlouse. He is panting heavily, exhaling a strong smell of cigarettes and

Murray Mints. They are similar in age, these two men, but Mr Priaulx's forty years of smoking make him look like another generation.

Yes? He waits for Mr Priaulx to catch his breath.

Two of the Year Twelves have gone, Mr Priaulx says. Run off somewhere.

Who?

Luc Batiste, Mr Priaulx says, and Gavin Mauger.

Where were they last seen? he asks, squinting across the headland. The clouds today are enormous, hulking. The weather on this island can change within a breath, especially in September.

Hard to say, Mr Priaulx says. Certainly at the start of the race. They were on the bus earlier, and we ticked them off on the register, but we haven't seen them since. None of the other students seem to know either. Should we alert their parents?

I think that we'd all like to avoid that, Mr Martel says, knowing full well how Mr Priaulx thrives on chaos. Whenever there's an asthma attack or a panic attack or a student gets their hand stuck in the drinks vending machine, there he is. Mr Martel would rather things were done without the whole student body whispering about what's happened, or without a journalist from the *Press* cornering him at the garage asking for a printable quote.

I bet they're sniffing glue, Mr Priaulx says. Or worse.

Or worse, Mr Martel repeats. Really. How long do we think they've been gone for?

Twenty minutes, maybe.

I see. I'll go first.

I could help—

No need for the search party just yet, he says. I'll call you in half an hour if I haven't found them.

He marches away from his colleagues towards the cliffs on the other side of the common. Luc Batiste probably is sniffing something somewhere, he knows. Mr Martel has previously caught him dealing wraps behind the hockey pavilion, and the police have asked about him on more than one occasion. He needs more evidence to enforce a permanent exclusion. He quickens his pace over the tufts of grass and clover.

The hawthorn is bare and the wind tousles the gorse. In the near distance, golfers are plodding across the members-only course that borders the common land, the turf cut in clean green curves against the tall bracken and nettles. He casts his eyes over the landscape, looking from the inland patch of scrub over to where it litters out by the sea wall. The only people on the beach are dog-walkers, and not even Luc Batiste's record of drug-dealing comes with the ingenuity of stealing a dog as a disguise. There is no movement from the dunes either, no smoke signal rising from a crafty cigarette. Soon, he has reached the end of the common and he pauses by the coastal path beside the concrete bunkers, breathing in the chilly air. The generous sands of Pembroke Bay below are the yellowest on the island. It is low tide. There is nothing, no one, on the sand other than a knotted blanket of sable seaweed. He looks inland again to where the gorse is matted in dark patches and tries to distinguish any possible hiding places. Perhaps they are shielding themselves in one of the headland's many tombs and tunnels.

Stone dolmens and menhirs are dotted across the common, part of the criss-cross of ancient tombs that have been dug into the north of the island. The darkness of these kinds of places is familiar to Mr Martel. He spent his childhood exploring the Nazi bunkers that had been carved and concreted into the island's cliffs. The fortifications are part of the landscape; unremarkable, unless you're a young boy looking for hiding places.

Yes, he thinks, looking at the mounds and stone markers of the ancient tombs, that's where he would hide if he were Luc right now. He walks a little further back up the path inland, and then pushes his way out into the unruly scrub. Brambles scratch at the sleeves of his anorak and at the ankles of his trousers.

At intervals, he shouts out for Luc and Gavin. The foliage plumps in the breeze but there doesn't seem to be anyone sheltering within the blackberry bushes. He can see the murky entrances to the main tombs as he approaches them now. A few more tussocks to clamber over, careful to avoid the thorns and nettles, and he will be at the opening of one of the ancient tunnels.

It's a shame, he thinks, that so many of his pupils are turning to aerosol tins when they could enjoy so many other things about living on an island. But he knows that he sounds like an old man when he tells them that.

The first tomb's entrance is gated and silted up with rubbish, empty crisp packets woven between the grimy cast-iron bars that surround the tomb's perimeter. He rests his hands on his waist while he catches his breath and then checks the gate's padlock. The lock is matted with oxidation, fused shut; they couldn't have got through this gate. He scrambles through the briar to find the entrance to the next tomb along, La Varde, the biggest of the burial sites, its entrance gaping open like a ghost train.

La Varde is dark and clammy inside, musked with the fetid warmth of a rabbit hutch. No signs of smoking, no cigarette butts on the dirt floor. He takes a step into the blackness, questioning whether the boys would really have had the shrewdness to skive off in a Stone Age dolmen. They'd have to have known it existed, for one, and neither Luc Batiste nor Gavin Mauger have been famed for their attention span in the classroom; one has a reputation for violence and dealing, the other for disrupting every lesson he attends.

Down here, hidden from the wind, the shouts from the school race cannot be heard. Mr Martel closes his eyes and opens them again, trying to adjust to the darkness. He resorts to using the torch on his phone, shining the ghostly light over the weathered stone walls of the tunnel. He can't remember if he came down here once on a school trip himself, when he was a boy and a pupil at the same school that he teaches at now.

He keeps walking, his footsteps the only sound in the stale gloom. His torch flashes on nothing in particular: chocolate bar wrappers, weeds, fox shit. There are no syringes to be seen, no crack pipes or blister packs, none of the tiny resealable plastic baggies that make him think of the spare button packets sewn into new coats. He can't see any of the paraphernalia that has been painstakingly demonstrated by the police on their school visits.

A grunt echoes from the darkness of the nearby burial chamber. This is followed by another grunt, and scuffling. He pauses, wondering if an act of violence is being committed and he should phone the police. The boys must be involved with older dealers. Or maybe one of the boys is choking on his own sick after inhaling too much solvent.

He can't yet be sure but something in him feels scared. The noise continues, and he tiptoes further down the shaft of the chamber towards the source of the noise. He turns off his torch, just in case. Perhaps, he thinks, his hands feeling along the rough stone walls, the two boys have found a dog lost on the common and they are now torturing it.

The grunts grow louder as he draws closer, lifting his shoes quietly on the earthen floor. He can hear breathing now. He reaches into his pocket for the phone again, and the white light of the torch flares in the chamber.

One of the boys is easy enough to recognise. He is bullish in the shoulders and neck, his fists heavy as hooves. He is entering the lower sixth this year, rising up through the body-odoured ranks like a prize swimmer fighting for air. Luc Batiste. And in his arms, their lips larded together, is Gavin Mauger.

Naked, dimpled skin popping with curls of recent hair; muscles taut and hands clamping at whatever flesh they can. All elbows and ribs. Their embrace has the energy of a punch-up, their running shorts writhing around their ankles. For the fierceness of it, Mr Martel is surprised by how little noise they are making.

He considers scuffing his feet on the dry dirt, or coughing and clearing his throat. Or shouting, as they are his students who ought to be doing cross-country right now. They certainly shouldn't be doing this in their school uniforms. They're in a public place, he thinks, and the law would be against them. Mr Martel knows that he should really inform the police. But he could also just walk straight back out into the creamy September light.

While he decides what his course of action should be,

he realises that he is still watching the pair of them. He is dumbfounded. Then he flashes the torchlight over them for lack of a better thing to do.

Luc Batiste looks up mid-kiss, his eyes open with his shining tongue still pushing in and out of his companion's mouth.

Mr Martel has witnessed students wetting themselves in detention, falling over dead-limbed after assemblies, having epileptic fits at carol services and in geography exams. But being party to two students engaging in mutual masturbation while they were meant to be running from Mont Cuet to Fort Le Marchant is not something he has previously experienced. Now that he finally has the pair's attention, as they hike up their running shorts and wipe the saliva from their chins, he doesn't know what to say.

Gavin Mauger has weaselled himself out of the embrace and is looking at his headteacher with fear and curiosity. Mr Martel has never seen either of these boys look afraid before.

You won't tell, will you, sir? Gavin says.

Mr Martel can hear his own sawtooth breathing cutting through the silence. It's probably unwise to call up the boys' parents, especially after the difficult meeting with the Batistes earlier that year. Detention doesn't seem apt. He thinks of the male teachers that the boys might have crushes on: self-satisfied Mr Goode, of course, and Mr Wilkes the drama teacher. How could he punish the boys without making their actions public knowledge? Of all the gossip that reaches the staff room, the tales of bunker parties and stomach pumpings and parents' divorces, never has a rumour about these two boys filtered through the coffee. There must be gay teenagers in his school, he knows, but their secret-keeping is apparently effective. In fact, in all his time as headteacher, the only one that he'd heard of was a Year 8 student who'd had his face hammered into the common-room lockers by, he remembers now, Luc Batiste. Luc had wiped the blood from his knuckles onto his school trousers while he was being told off, shrugging and refusing to say sorry. But now, Mr Martel understands that he doesn't want the boys to feel as if they have done something wrong.

Can we go? Luc says.

Get back to the race, Mr Martel snaps. Get out. Now. Get out.

Gavin Mauger goes first, scuttling back through the tunnel towards the daylight, his shoelaces clicking on the floor. Luc Batiste trails behind, no urgency in his step. He turns round and looks at his teacher, eyes glistening like spit in the darkness. Then he goes too.

Mr Martel stays there in the subterranean quiet for one minute, two. The beam of his torch has dropped to the floor. He gives the boys a head start before he carefully winds his way back along the uneven ground towards the fresh air. The wind is sharp on his skin, the sky bright grey like a computer screen so that he has to blink several times to adjust. The jeers from the cross-country race can be heard across the briar and bracken. He doesn't feel very well, like he might faint or soil himself, he doesn't know which. Instead of returning immediately to his colleagues, he paces the short walk eastwards towards the block of public toilets nestled under the blond wing of Pembroke Bay.

The tiled outbuilding thrums with bleach and urine. He bungs up the middle sink with basic-grade toilet roll and fills it to the brim with cold water. He splashes it over his blooming neck and face, his sickness subsiding a little. A flush sounds from one of the other toilets and he catches his own surprise in the mottled mirror.

Flecks of toilet roll slime the creases in between his fingers but he doesn't bother wasting time drying his hands: he strides straight back out into the ruffling wind, wet hands in his pockets. He makes his way through the kiosk car park, along the sea wall, past the concrete bunkers and gun slits, up the scraggy path that leads away from the bay. Then over the path, across the ruffling tufts of gorse and grass, past the dark cubbyholes of dolmens and bunkers.

The happiest summer of his life was the one he'd spent on his sixth-form German exchange in Bonn. The family fed him well, he went on day trips. He perfected his vocab in the nearby state school, and he slept in the same room as the boy who would become his first lover. Pieter. Days and nights together, hot breath under the cold sheets each evening and the thrill of getting back to his own bed before his host-mother knocked on the door to wake them up for class the next morning. The headrush that came with having such a secret: they had felt as if they were winning at a game. When it came for Pieter to stay with Mr Martel's own family in Guernsey, his parents eyed the boy with disgust that went beyond the Nazi Occupation that they had lived through. The school had said that it would be a challenge for some families to live with a German for a week, and that it was an exercise in community-building and forgiveness as much as linguistic education, but he saw spite as much as suspicion in his parents' behaviour. His mother had made him sleep on a camp bed on the floor of his sister's bedroom, beside her, and Pieter slept in his own room, alone. He wondered if Pieter had nosed around his things, gone through his drawers, read his diary; he had hoped so.

Mr Martel hasn't thought of Pieter in years; he has certainly tried not to. It wasn't legalised on the island until well after he'd got married and had children, not until over a decade after the laws had changed on the mainland even. By then, Mr Martel had cloistered himself with the routine of feature-length historical dramas on Friday nights, Saturday clifftop walks and coffees at the Gouffre, trips to the Friquet plant nursery on a Sunday. He thinks how much his wife Hilary would enjoy being out on the headland today, pointing out the hardy wildflowers and the mosses. As he now approaches his teaching colleagues, who are clustered together against the cold weather while the students haul themselves over the race's finish line, he finds the swell of memory hard to shore up. His pulse is thick with it.

Mr Priaulx turns around at Mr Martel's approach and he worries if there is something in his appearance that has given away his discomfort. He turns around and checks that there is nobody behind him, scanning the horizon that is seemingly empty.

They've turned up finally by themselves, Mr Priaulx says. You didn't see them?

No, Mr Martel says.

Shame, Mr Priaulx says. You could've got rid of them for good.

He nods, and when Mr Priaulx has turned his attention back to the runners, he glances over at the staff and jogging students. The students are sweating even in the cold, straggling over the white strip of tape laid on the mud to mark the finish line. Luc Batiste and Gavin Mauger are walking next to some other boys who have slopped a bright blue energy drink down their white polo shirts. They don't look at Mr

Martel as they pass by. The event takes another half-hour to fully finish, at which point he reads out the names of the winners from a scrap of paper and hands out a clutch of cheap medals. He waves at a few smiling parents but moves off to the car park before they can approach him.

The car feels oddly quiet after the bluster of the headland and the race. He switches the radio on, turning up a Porter tune that he likes very much. It wheedles about going home to someone and how nice a thing that would be. Mr Martel can't bring himself to sing along even though he knows the words and can pick out the melody on the piano at home. The car park empties around him. Next on is that raucous tune from *Cabaret*, sung in a voice too loud and shrill. He had never been convinced by Michael York in the film, Mr Martel thinks, remembering how he'd sat in the cinema thinking wistfully of a Weimar Germany like Isherwood's. Real life didn't really have its cleavage out, glittering, like that. He listens to the song in full before snatching on the car ignition and driving in the direction of the school, rather than home. He parks in the reserved space with HEADTEACHER sprayed in big white letters on the tarmac. The students and the rest of the staff won't bother to return after the race, and the school is empty now.

The hot chocolate vending machine hums as he spirits through the empty reception area. He closes the door to his office and seats himself behind his desk, just as he might do on a Monday morning with teaching in full session. He'd like to speak to someone but he can't think of anyone appropriate. The numbers on his speed dial are his home landline, his wife's mobile number, the news desk of the local paper. Mr Martel feels that his wife would be confused if he recounted the day's events to her. She wouldn't understand why he hadn't punished the boys, especially as he'd been looking for a way to get rid of Luc Batiste for good for so long now. Why didn't you stop them, she would say? Shouldn't you report it to the police? Their parents? Do they have something over you, you're not in trouble? The callous thought crosses his mind that sometimes his wife knows nothing about anything, and although he is aware of the cruelty in the idea, in this case he feels it's partly true.

He calls home. Hilary, he says, over the sound of a pan lid clanking. She has started to enjoy cooking more and more during her retirement, teaching herself new skills and buying wooden-handled Japanese knives and special sushi mats. She frequently tells him that when he retires, he will find things to do that he will love too. They will go on more holidays abroad, maybe even a cruise, and spend more time in each other's company. Mr Martel has eighteen months left until then.

I'm just cooking, she says. There's a chicken in, are you on your way?

I'll be half an hour, he says. I have to pop round the office on the way back to pick something up.

Righto, she says. I'll hold off on the peas.

She hangs up, and so does he. He looks around the room at the shelves that are lined with other people's achievements. He's seen enough students grow into adults and parents, and grandparents even, to know that not everyone achieves everything they thought that they could. He knows that people get lonely and old and sorry; how they regret having been a stranger to themselves. He didn't think it would be him. The realisation comes like a twisted ankle near the end of the race.

He thinks now of the look on his mother's face when she caught him holding hands with Pieter in the lane on the walk home from school, on what would be Pieter's first and last visit to the Channel Islands. Of how Pieter had plucked his hand away as if he'd touched the hotplate on the Rayburn, leaving Mr Martel – or Sam, as he was then – holding nothing but shame and rejection. Of how he wanted to speed up that evening, week, year; of how he wanted to speed through the rest of his life to get away from the hurt of it. He thinks of his two students today, terrors that they are, kissing as if time would run out in the darkness of the dolmen.

Pigs

St Peter Port, 2013

Jen had been a bully at school so it was only natural that she went into the police, she'd always joke. Sod university, she'd say about her teenage decision, she'd start on a decent salary and wouldn't have to work out what to wear every day, plus she'd get to drive a car well over the island's paltry speed limit and nick the people who annoyed her most. She'd wear black bras under her white blouse and walk down the street with a wink in her arse.

Except whatever she said to her colleagues in the pub, she knew that people didn't respect the police here. She'd been one of their lot before, pissing on doorsteps all along the Pollet and laughing at ID notices, and she can't believe she thought it would be any different for her on the other side. Pigs, porkos. People honked at her in the street. Children threw bacon rashers at her patrol vehicle and then, when they found out where she lived in the phonebook, at her front door. Eggs too, on occasion. She gave up on singing at open mic nights at the town pubs, gave up on dating. Justice wasn't the original reason she'd signed up for the job but a handful of years in, she was beginning to understand the feeling of injustice.

It was not a bad place to be a police officer, but she found it boring compared to the mainland news reports of armed robberies and homicides. Domestic abuse and heroin possession and parking tickets were among Guernsey's prime crop of crimes. The island's few homeless were routinely offered cells and hot meals for the night, and prostitution was left to the experts. The one time that a body was found hacked up in the park, the whole station staff queued up in their squad cars to take turns gawking at the corpse and sicking up in the nearby bin. Jen had never expected policing to be fun but the recruitment adverts had reliably claimed that it was varied, lively. She was beginning to think that it was just a job like any other. Without murders and missing children, there was little to do but yell at thirteen-year-olds getting off in Saumarez Park. Each day was becoming such a drag.

There's been another disturbance up by Les Capelles, the desk clerk told Jen as she slunk inside for her shift. The neighbours are reporting a lot of noise. Shouting. A woman, early thirties. Her partner left after an argument sometime around eight this morning.

As one of the few female officers, Jen often got given the home visits. She found herself nodding cow-eyed at wives with alcoholic husbands and sons and cousins. She would make them tea, chase up the paramedics if the bleeding hadn't stopped. Meanwhile her patrol partner Jason would sit in the car eating custard horns and dialling in to Island FM's competitions in the hope that a thousand-pound cash win would buy him out of the job. He was gunning to go to Thailand, he'd explain, or at least Berlin because they had nightclubs with more than one dancefloor there. Jason liked trance music and the convenience of living at home. He said he didn't like crying women. Today Jen didn't much feel like them either.

Is there nothing else? Jen said. You're always giving me these.

The clerk said that a patrol needed back-up with a kid who had run away from school with a lunchbox packed full of resin. She could have the job as long as she drove up to the housing estate near Les Capelles afterwards and had a look in, she was sure it could wait. If the partner's already gone out, it can't get worse.

After all, disturbances were common at this address, a close owned by the States that was well hidden from the tourists and the tax evaders. Burglaries, black eyes, dogs chewing through car seats and children; Jen knew that the wild rumours were prejudiced and unhelpful, but she still felt anxious about going there. The police were not welcome. Jen left the station with a flurry of relief that there was a valid reason to avoid the case for a few hours at least.

I'll call you if you're needed sooner, the desk clerk said.

Cheerie, said Jen, signing out the squad car.

Jason treated them to a rush on the blue siren and raced down the high-hedged lanes with their colourful array of pay-what-you-can vegetable boxes perched on walls and gateposts. They overtook cyclists and cut up slow-moving Citroëns with French number plates. A bus driver shouted through his window that the police were worse than criminals with road etiquette like that. They drove on to Bordeaux, a grey beach littered with dark pebbles and boats tugging against their corroded chains like pit bulls. Two other police cars were parked outside the kiosk, their officers standing beside them, fleeced against the grim wind. Another officer was winching a motorboat off a trailer, which grated over the shingle into the steely water. Jen was about to ask what the boat was needed for when she saw the splashing beyond the shoreline.

He's got a couple of ounces of cannabis resin clingfilmed to his chest, one of her colleagues explained. He's still a teenager. Good pocket money. It'll go to waste in the water like that. What a moron.

Jen sidled up to her male colleagues, who were blowing on their knuckles to keep them warm, while Jason went off to the kiosk for a microwaved cheese and onion pasty. The swimming figure in the distance was making little headway against the dark current, the waves gritting over him every other stroke. The white collar of his school shirt flashed like a seabird as he struggled on.

Why's he swimming? Jen asked.

Beats me. We were running after him over the dunes and he just went on into the water, her colleague said. Maybe we shouldn't have had the handcuffs out so quick, eh. Scared him off. He'll get tired sooner or later; we'll pick him up then.

Jason returned with pastry flaked down his pullover and grease pooled on his lower lip. He wittered on about tide times and unfavourable wind speeds. Jason surfed at the weekends when he wasn't on duty, something Jen had once tried and given up on as quickly as she'd given up on making friends among her colleagues. She'd had a laugh with them at first, shared the odd pint down the pub after a shift. She could match them in rounds and chip in with bullish anecdotes. It wasn't that she was prudish, or precious. But lately she just wanted to skip through to the end of the conversations, like fast-forwarding through the adverts.

Will we reel him in now, Sergeant? Or will we wait? one of the men asked, clipping together the salt-stiffened clasps of his lifejacket over his uniform. The rubber dinghy rasped eagerly on the shingle, strings of kelp browning its orange underbelly.

See how far towards France he gets, was the superior's reply.

Jason laughed, something he always did at the guvnor's jokes, and coughed up some scalding potato purée onto the pebbles. The local paper sometimes accused the police of being lazy but really Jason was after entertainment as much as anyone else. A sea arrest – or rescue, Jen thought – would make for a great afternoon out as well as a good newspaper headline. More officers than were necessary clambered into the dinghy, its oilskin puffed out against the water, and they thrummed the motor against the tide towards the young swimmer in the distance. Jen watched from the shoreline.

There was talk of putting bets on how many miles out the spluttering boy could crawl for. The motorboat teased behind him, the officers smug at the impending arrest. It wasn't a fair fight but then a teenager trying to smuggle and shift drugs on the island wasn't right in the head, the men said, especially if he thought swimming away from juvenile prison was a viable way out. He wouldn't get as far as Herm, nor Brecqhou, not even the snagged outcrops of rocks where the puffins perched in high season. Jen shivered and looked across to France skulking in the distance, fog descending on its brow. The sea could be bitter in summer but even the fish wouldn't be out today.

The boy was writhing from the cold when they finally tipped him ashore. The first thing the sergeant did was to rip the resin package from his chest. The kid heaved on the pebbles, red-cheeked from exertion and embarrassment. A twenty-one-year-old constable from St Sampson's, who claimed to be the boy's cousin, lightly kicked his bum. The policemen all laughed, cheered. This would be a front-page news story in *The Guernsey Press*, one that might even get them a free round of ciders in The Parrot that night. The boy started to cry then and he looked even younger.

Get the kid a blanket, will you, the sergeant said to Jen.

Jen went to fetch the emergency foil blanket from the boot of the squad car. She found the packet but it was empty inside. She grabbed the empty plastic and held it up to Jason with an accusing look.

It was cold out surfing and Davo forgot his wetsuit, Jason said with a shrug. What? Oh come on, because you wouldn't?

No, I wouldn't actually, Jen said.

Jason made an ooh-ooh noise.

Jen clinked up the beach towards the kiosk for a length of tinfoil to wrap around the boy's juddering shoulders. The vendor let her inside with the smile of a man who still found women being in the police a novelty. He knelt down beside the boxes of outdated ketchup sachets while he rummaged for the requisite roll of foil. Pasties hummed on the hotplate. She wondered how long they'd been reheating for, whether there had been any tourists in the area all day. Fog was starting to sidle up to the windows. Two o'clock and the afternoon already blackening. Jen could feel her lips splitting at the idea of visiting a claustrophobic flat in Les Capelles with energy-saving lights on in the daytime and someone in distress. She couldn't stand the thought of another story like that.

Cushy job you've got, the vendor said. You didn't even have to get your feet wet.

The vendor handed over the tinfoil and congratulated Jen on the successful arrest. It's good they're ridding the community of scum like that, he explained, especially now they're starting at such a young age. Get rid of the estates, that'll teach them. Send in the bailiffs if they can't pay their medical bills, everyone else has to. My wife's got a hyperactive thyroid and do you think it's easy for us?

Sorry to hear about that, I appreciate that must be difficult for you, Jen said. It was a phrase she used a lot for work, most days in fact. She wasn't sure if she'd ever said it outside of the job.

They should keep them out of the schools so they can't poison the children who want to work hard, the man went on. My granddaughter got an A in her ICT exam. Can you imagine?

Jen quietly thanked the man and crunched back across the beach towards her waiting colleagues. They shut the boy in the back of the van, foil crimped across his chest, his miserable figure shining through the tinted windows like some sort of celebrity. Jen gave him a wave as they drove off. He didn't return it.

Jen had volunteered for her and Jason to visit the boy's headteacher to inform him of the afternoon's outcome, as going to the school at least meant putting off the next call-out for another hour. They would explain to the headteacher the seriousness of the incident and the likelihood that the boy would have to appear before the upstanding community

members of the Jurat. The size of the drugs package had
signified an intent to deal, she would say. There may need
to be a raid on school premises and extra rounds of PSHE
lessons with dummy pipes and needles.

Jen could do the talking, they agreed. But now they could
see road signs for the school at the traffic lights, she could
feel the words snarking in her throat at the thought of classrooms and detention slips. Driving past her old school on
a daily basis was one thing, but re-entering its locker-lined
corridors was another.

The playing fields were full of shrieks and short skirts as
they pulled up outside. The smokers with their short ties
didn't move from the wall as Jen and Jason clumped past in
their regulation black shoes, pretending not to see so that
they wouldn't have to tell them off. Jen had smoked her way
through secondary school, smoked her way out of French lessons and smoked during history field trips, but she'd always
done it out of sight of the teachers. The blocked fire exit
behind the gymnasium had been privy to her smoking habit,
sexual prowess, slanging matches. She wondered whether it
still existed and why these teenagers weren't there now.

Can you smell bacon? one kid shouted.

An empty Lilt can vaulted past Jen's shoulder. Even Jason
was too nervous to snap at them, having been at the same
school not three years before.

Have you come back to see the careers adviser? another
kid jeered.

The duo ascended the concrete steps to the entrance
without looking back at the sneering crowd. The school had
been redeveloped several times in the years since Jen had left;
she had hoped not to recognise the interior of the entrance

but the polystyrene ceiling tiles and bull-ringed vending machines remained the same. The smell of powdered hot chocolate and armpits. They sat in reception as if waiting for a parent to pick them up on a sick day.

The headteacher will be with you soon, the receptionist explained. It was more a threat than a reassurance.

Jen had sat outside the headteacher's office more times than she'd left the island. The old treacle and feathers trick, laxatives and clingfilm, tampons spiked with bicarbonate of soda, and those thrilling punches where the flesh peeled away beneath her knuckles. She might have failed her written English exams but give her gossip about a classmate's stepmother or cousin, and she could twist words into fists. Detentions were numerous but she was careful not to go far enough to get expelled. She still had the faint blue lines on her left forearm from where she'd tattooed her victories with a compass point and fountain pen, fight wins scored like a barcode on her skin.

The problem was that once she'd started winning every fight she picked, she couldn't help herself. The first, she remembered well: she'd smacked Vicky Carey around the mouth for calling her a slag. The impact of the insult had lessened when half the common room started cheering on her behalf, calling her a lad and a fucking legend. The act bought her friends, drinks, weekends out of the house. But a tough reputation like that stuck, and needed regular upkeep. The memory of Vicky spitting out blood on the carpet tiles had stuck too.

Now Jen picked at the ripped edge of her thumbnail, looking at the annual school photos and engraved shields pinned along the wall. A late student clattered past towards the classrooms. The headteacher was keeping them waiting for longer than they'd anticipated and Jen wondered whether he knew who she was. The receptionist certainly did. It was hard to stop being the person you were at school when everyone you went to school with still lived in the same place.

They weren't offered tea when they were called inside. The office was smaller than she had remembered, a rectangular white room with its own kettle and miniature fridge. Mr Martel looked much the same, neat and tired. Once, when she'd commented in class on his hair looking like the colour of piss, he had patiently explained that these visible signs of stress were simply because of time-wasting pupils like her.

I expect you don't remember me, Jen said.

I never forget a single pupil, Jennifer, Mr Martel replied.

Jason said nothing, his hands pooled inside his trouser pockets and a smirk across his lips, so Jen went on as routinely as she could.

Has Luc shown signs of drug abuse before? she asked, making notes in her small flip notebook. Are there signs of drug use in the toilets or the locker rooms? Would it be helpful perhaps if we delivered an assembly about addiction and the long-term risks next week?

She explained that there wasn't much they could do for the boy because of the large quantity of cannabis found incontestably on his person, and that swimming away from the police had worsened his case. He already had a few counts on his record so if it wasn't this time, it'd be next. Unfortunately they'd seen juveniles on this path before, and it wouldn't be long before he would be classed as an adult. Mr Martel didn't reply so Jen said that she could leave some leaflets and that they'd better be on their way.

You know, I was initially very pleased when I heard you'd decided to go into the police, Mr Martel said. I thought it might do you good.

Right, Jen said. Sir.

Mr Martel paused for a long time before adding, I think it would be best if I telephoned Luc Batiste's parents myself, thank you. And we won't be needing an assembly.

Jason laughed at Jen all the way down the school steps. There they sat in the car park, Jen feeling the colour sting her cheeks and chest. Island FM was already reporting the boy's arrest with every drip of detail they could wring out of it. It was nearly time for Jason's favourite phone-in competition. He was talking through his Chiang Mai backpacking route ideas when the clerk radioed in that there had been another call about the flat disturbance from earlier. What had been screaming this morning was now sobbing and retching, and the neighbours couldn't get in, or didn't want to. Would Jen go and calm the woman down and see what was going on?

Dinner from the Chinese takeaway on the Rohais sat hot in Jen's lap while Jason drove them to the northern parishes. The afternoon's fog had moved inland so that houses stood headless and the other cars vanished in front of them along La Vrangue. The clerk radioed again to say an ambulance would be on the scene shortly, as a neighbour had called about a suspected overdose or fit. Jen put on her hat as they pulled up outside the estate. Jason would follow upstairs in ten minutes, he said, he just wanted to park the car somewhere it wouldn't get trashed.

The low-level houses of the estate shone like teeth under the streetlights. You had to get right up close to the doors to see the numbers. At the station there had long been talk of police getting egged by kids down by the bins, so Jen listened carefully for the tell-tale squeak of running trainers before approaching the buzzer for the flat. She buzzed. Nothing. She buzzed again.

The door was unlocked when Jen pushed it. Picking up the thick slew of post from the doormat, she recognised the name printed on a credit card bill. She checked the other letters. All of them were typed with a name that she herself had written over and over again in her teenage diary, on Christmas card envelopes and forged sickness notes: Kathryn Renouf. She wished that the clerk on the front desk had been able to give her her name beforehand. Jen pushed through the dark hallway into the sticky warmth of the flat and caught sight of herself in a mirror, her uniform squared on her hefty shoulders. She tried not to look so scared.

The ambulance was meant to get here first, Jen said when she saw the mess. It's on its way. How are you doing there, Kat?

The woman was slumped on the floor beside the sofa, the hair on her cheek yellowed with sick and wetted with whatever spirits she'd been drinking. Jen took a step closer, careful to avoid the toy farm that was sprawled in front of the fake fireplace.

Kat said nothing, her eyes coasting over Jen. They hadn't seen each other properly since school, when they had been best friends in the way that only teenage girls could be. Calling each other the moment they got through the door after school, passing notes in maths, sharing the same skirts, cigarettes and boyfriends. Their parents knew each other's names from the weekends they had to spend ratting out the lies their daughters had told about sleepovers and house parties. Their final summer of friendship, the August before Kat followed some bloke to the mainland for a short-lived stint, they had plundered the town pubs' remaining virgins and laughed at their sobbing girlfriends. It was easier to do things like that when there were two of you.

The first time Kat was back on the rock for Christmas, the steam smutting up the windows inside the De La Rue with Noddy Holder railing loudly in the loos, she had sniggered to see Jen working behind the bar. Jen had been nineteen then, bulky-chested and unworried, calling back to the cat-callers and fucking builders in car parks after her shift. She hadn't felt ashamed of herself till Kat that night told her that she should be. Kat gave her a fifty-pence tip out of the change from her Jack and Coke and they didn't speak again. Jen joined the police that January. It was easier to feel that she was doing something with her life when she had a uniform to show for it.

What's happened here? Jen tried again, moving closer towards Kat. I need you to tell me what's going on.

When Kat didn't reply, Jen radioed the station to check that the ambulance was on its way. Yes, she would put the individual in the recovery position if she lost consciousness and yes, she would keep her airway clear in case she started vomiting. She'd done it for this woman before, just a long time ago, back when she would've still called her a girl.

Kat had short hair now, not the straightened, highlighted sheet of blonde that she used to scowl behind. Kat coughed up into the empty ice-cream tub that Jen handed her while she surveyed the flat. It was the part of the job that Jen had always secretly enjoyed, seeing inside other people's houses, but today the sight made her throat twinge. Few photos, piles of magazines. Washing was draped on the radiators, stretched leggings and baby bibs with towelled tigers and elephants smiling at the scene. The smell of laundry softener palled under the pinch of vodka, which had emptied from its bottle over the beige carpet. Two dozen untaken white pills were dissolving into the wet matting.

The fucking state you're in, Jen stopped herself from saying out loud. Instead she put her arms under Kat's and shifted her upright, setting her knees tight to her chest. She could feel Kat's shinbones, thin and flat, through her skinny jeans. She was light to hold. Jen wiped her hands on her regulation navy trousers and tightly screwed back the cap on the vodka bottle, putting its remaining clear quarter far out of reach. She'll be all right after she gets her stomach pumped, Jen thought; it wasn't so serious. Only sad, and tedious.

She remembered that when they were teenagers, they had each downed a pint of orange juice after a pint of milk in the hope of chucking up before the cross-country race. The volcanic trick hadn't worked and they'd been forced by Mrs Le Noury to run across the rabbit-holed cliffs anyway, the acidic mix slopping around beneath their polo shirts and crotch-cutting gym knickers. One of them had twisted an ankle although their actions were so interchangeable in memory that Jen wasn't sure if it was her or Kat who'd ended up in A&E that day. Most of her teenage memories were like that, sick-smeared and migraine-coloured. If she carried on like this, perhaps her adult memories would be the same. She hadn't stayed close with anyone from school, hadn't thought any of their peers worth keeping up with back then, and now it made her smart to see their close-knit groups drinking cider in the pubs and eating out at the latest places in town.

She dreaded making small talk with the people she had once bullied and who were apparently now living full and content lives. Maybe they would be nice to her but she dreaded that too. She found it easier to talk to strangers who had had a break-in or got drunk and driven into the sea wall; they never asked her what she was doing on the weekend. Looking at Kat now, it was hard to imagine that there had been a time when Saturday nights were spent at parties and not watching live singing contests on television with a takeaway.

Can you tell me what you've taken? Are they just the one type of painkiller or have you been mixing drugs? What are these little ones here?

Kat spat out a mouthful of bile without taking her eyes off her.

Jen trudged through to the small kitchen where the fog was peering in through the windows. She couldn't see any labelled blister packs or pill bottles. She opened the bin, which revealed nothing unusual. There were no clues on the worktop and the fridge was empty except for doll-sized jars of puréed apple and Petit Filous. There was a baby's bottle washed up on the sideboard, its three body parts carefully separated and turned up to dry. Jen returned to the lounge and looked at Kat crumpled on the floor, then went to the brown-tiled bathroom, and the bedroom with make-up greased across the bedspread and fairy lights hanging from the mirror. The cot in the corner was empty.

Where's the baby? Jen asked, her voice too loud in the small flat.

Kat laughed at this and retched again. Jen waited without a smile.

You've not done anything stupid, have you?

She's with her dad, Kat said. We had a fight.

Do you often have fights?

Who doesn't?

Well, Jen said. What were you fighting about this time?

Like you care.

It's my job to ask.

Exactly.

Jen knelt down beside her while they waited for the ambulance. Jason would be on his way soon too, Jen knew, locking
the car remotely and running up two steps at a time. He
doubtless wouldn't notice the toy farm laid out in its careful
rows as he came in. The black eyes of small plastic cows and
sheep stared blankly across the stained carpet. They were
unevenly painted so that some of the animals had disconcert-
ing peach-coloured patches on their full bellies and rumps, as
if stricken with a skin disease. Jen knew they were just cheap.

You'll be okay, Jen said.

I couldn't do it properly, Kat said. I couldn't. I didn't know
you have to take so many.

Jen put her hand on Kat's. They sat like that for a while,
waiting. She could feel Kat's pulse ticking through her shallow palms. She wanted to ask if Kat ever thought about her
when Lauryn Hill came on the radio, or if she remembered
the time they'd snuck into Amy Falla's sixteenth birthday
party with gin-filled Fruit Shoot bottles stuffed down their
cowboy boots. Jen had heard that things had gone badly for
Kat since moving back to the island, but she'd never heard
why and now it felt too late to ask.

Are you sure I can't do anything for you?

To her relief, Kat nodded and squeezed her hand. Can I
try a bit of tea?

Well, Jen said. I'm not meant to give you anything to drink, but ...

Please, Kat said. I think it'll make me feel better.

With a crack of her knees, Jen returned to the kitchen and topped up the kettle, the limescale crunching as she forced the lid shut. The wheeze as it began to boil masked her sigh. She was tired now and could feel the cold from the beach creeping in as she leaned on the chipped melamine of the sideboard. The grimy white cupboards were pearlised by the light coming from the stacks of parallel flats outside the uncurtained window. Shouts from kids and parents and televisions echoed through the huddle of buildings. No sign of the ambulance siren yet, although sometimes the emergency services turned them off when parking up here, not wanting to draw unnecessary attention. The kettle clicked off and Jen made the tea, heaping in an extra spoonful of sugar for Kat to keep her energy up. She knew she wasn't meant to give Kat anything to drink, had been strictly told in her first-aid training not even to give water, but that wasn't the point. Maybe they could go for a drink some day, or she could invite Kat round once the weather was nice, and they could sit in the garden and talk. She closed her palms around the two hot cups and returned to the lounge.

She could hear the terrible noise before she'd rounded the sofa. Kat was gurgling. Face-forward in her own sick, vodka bottle uncapped and now empty, red carpet stipples on her knees and forearms. All of the leftover pills had gone. Her eyes were slack, her legs shining with urine. Jen knelt in the scalding tea she'd slopped in shock and slapped Kat's face, slapped her arms, heaved at her chest. Jen clawed away the whey dribble of pills and sick from Kat's mouth and laid her heavy wet limbs in the recovery position.

It wasn't until Jason and the ambulance men lurched inside, miniature cows and hedges and pigs and ducks cleaving underfoot, that she realised she was sobbing. She stepped back while the men strapped the unconscious body to the trolley, taking care not to bang the wheels on the railings as they shifted it along the unlit corridor and down the pavement. Neighbours watched from their kitchens and bedrooms. Jen went back into the empty flat to check she'd left nothing behind, and took the opportunity to wipe her cheeks. She set the two now-empty mugs upright on the table, the tea pooled darkly across the floor, and went to the bedroom to pack an overnight bag for Kat.

GIRLS GIRLS GIRLS

St Helier, 2014

I don't know why we couldn't just stay in Guernsey, Becky said as they left the restaurant.

There aren't any proper strip clubs in Guernsey, Claire said. Brian said the ones here are better.

Brian said that?

Come on, Claire said, giving Nikki a slap on her arse as if she were a cow blocking a country lane.

I feel a bit funny about strippers, Nikki said.

Me too, said Annie.

Think how impressed your Marc will be when you tell him, Claire said to Nikki, steadying her on her bevel-edged feet and straightening her I'M GETTING HITCHED sash. He'll be so turned on you won't even have to have sex with him. He'll love you for it. Anyway, you couldn't have a hen do in Guernsey. Can you imagine?

It would be a laugh. The whole weekend away in Jersey was a laugh – Nikki was getting married after all. They would find the club as easily as if it sported a Las Vegas-style fluorescent sign complete with flashing tits and flamingo thighs. They'd step inside the shadowy club and laugh all the old perverts off their bar stools. They would laugh along with the lapdancers, get up on the podiums and do the Macarena. Down Baileys and tequila shots and find themselves back on the flight home tomorrow with hangovers worthy of weeks of storytelling. They would all wink at each other during the wedding speeches in the knowledge that Nikki had had the best night of her unmarried life. Surely.

After asking a cashier in an off-licence for directions, they made their way down the cobbled streets of St Helier, careful to hold hands against any falls. Their heels clacked, echoing in the darkness, the old town rising up around them. Tourist couples were dining on early-bird menus in the windows of seafood restaurants and the takeaways were turning up the heat on their fryers. There were few cars in the back streets. The shops thinned out and unwelcoming pubs appeared on every corner. Nikki needed the toilet so the three other girls shielded her from a passing man while she crouched on the pavement and pissed between her silver stilettos. Claire held on to Nikki's hands to keep her balance as she squatted. A rivulet ran down the street in the direction of a pair of necking teenagers, perched on their mopeds with helmets cradled in their arms like children.

You wouldn't do that at home, Becky said.

She's not at home, she's on holiday, Claire said. Jersey's a dump, anyway.

Shithole, Nikki said, wiping herself with a Nivea face wipe.

Parts of it are quite nice, I thought, said Annie. No?

When they reached the rumoured strip club, cash at the

ready and tongues already furring from the empty gin-in-a-tins in their hands, they were surprised not to find a bouncer on the door. The place had the right name, *Whispers*, but the door looked more like that of a gig venue than a burlesque boutique. DJ names and 2-4-1 drinks offers were stamped on shiny posters. The door opened onto a steep, shadowed staircase that they descended, arm in arm, delicate as a daisy chain. Inside, the club looked even less like the strip club that the girls had been imagining. The working women were in tank tops and fluted miniskirts rather than matching PVC thongs and cage bras. There were no schoolgirl uniforms to be seen. There were no poles of note. Two kittens mewled amongst the bins of empties on the floor like toddlers in a supermarket.

Does this look right to you? Becky said, looking around for a DJ or the tell-tale sign of a discarded nipple tassel.

I don't see why not, Claire replied. Such was the duty of a bridesmaid on a hen do: to be happy at all times.

The air con blasted the stench from the steamed-up toilets towards the bar stools so the girls decided to find seats in a more secluded location. They swayed across the treacly floor to a booth quilted with red leatherette. There they set up camp, piling their handbags up in one corner and spreading their spending money and lipsticks across the sticky tabletop. It was early still, the barmaids stocking up the back-mirrored bar and slicing unwashed lemons.

Drinks, Claire announced.

I've never been in a strip club before, Nikki said. I'm so excited now we're here.

So excited, Annie said.

I'll get us a round of shots, Claire said.

I don't like sambuca, Becky said. Aniseed repeats on me.

Well I fucking love sambuca, Claire said, striding towards the bar with the tightness of her dress lacerating her armpits. The compression over her stomach made her think of the diagrams of corsets in school history textbooks, showing women's organs being reshaped like sausage-meat. Claire shouted behind her, You can choose the booze when you buy the next round.

Claire did love sambuca, it was true. She loved Jägermeister, gin and Corky's flavoured shots, and she always paid her way. She drank glowing Aperol spritzes with the girls after work, rosé with Brian when they were cooking dinner. She was prized at work parties for being able to drink as well as any of the finance boys. She loved the familiar feeling that came at a certain point in the evening, as if she was plummeting out of the mundane. She loved it with a reggae heart and an open throat, tears in her eyes and horror reeling in her stomach. The world had felt full of jagged edges until Claire discovered how well drink softened it up: she didn't have to be so precious all the time.

Claire spread the requisite pound notes out on the bar and bought eight shots for her and her friends. The server behind the bar sloshed the liqueur between the shot glasses without taking her eyes off Claire's cleavage, which had darkened dramatically between her breasts where the fake tan had drip-dried. Claire crossed her arms in front of her chest until the tacky tray of drinks was ready. The group cheered at the sight of the spirits, and Annie made a limp gesture to do with party poppers; Nikki smiled and that was all that mattered.

The four of them had been at school together, had learned

hopscotch and kissing rhymes and French together. Their friendships had survived numerous rows and rumours and factions, but what had always mattered was that they had grown up, and now lived, in the same place. It was impossible for Claire to imagine living on Guernsey without sharing drinks and cabs with these women. Claire looked at her friends, their ombré eyeshadow and jellied bra-boosters sparkling in the half-light, and really could not imagine it.

Becky was shifting around in her seat as if to make a point about how much room the four of them had in the near-empty bar. The gel-covered spotlights revealed only men on their own in corners and a huddle of underage French exchange students. Claire had to admit, the atmosphere was worse than on her own hen do, for which the girls had gone to The Island Bowl and got laughed at by the teenagers hanging out in the car park. The families trying to have a nice Saturday night out had eyed the boozing hens with disdain, while the teenagers had pestered them to buy them alcohol every time they went to the bar. Claire couldn't remember being that pushy at her age but Becky had jeered that yes, Claire had been asking for alcopops for as long as time.

Now, the claustrophobia was settling in on her shoulders for the night. Becky was biting her lips, ready to complain; over the past few months, the bride-to-be's wishes had become a war of attrition. Annie stepped back from potential arguments to let Claire and Becky fight it out between them. So Claire now raised a cheers to Nikki and went off to get the next round: she could at least prove her status as a bridesmaid by providing the drinks.

Becky didn't earn as much, Claire knew, and hated having to keep up with the others. Becky had a husband who was tight-fisted and undersexed and if Claire wasn't enjoying her own marriage, Becky was having even less fun. Claire bought them all two more rounds of shots. Becky protested at the sambuca again but they slogged back their two shots each, whooping Nikki for having found the love of her life. What a miracle to find the perfect soulmate on an island with a population of only sixty-odd thousand. Nikki, Claire, Becky: they had all found husbands within the small shoreline. Annie was still struggling with her search for a boyfriend but dating could be difficult, so Becky repeatedly told her, if you weren't realistic.

Why don't we find you a guy tonight? Claire soothed.

No, tonight's all about Nikki, Becky said.

One of us might as well get laid, Nikki said. Isn't that what you said, Becks, once you get married, you might as well darn it over?

Piss off was that me.

Go on. It's not like you can have a one-nighter on Guernsey if you don't want the whole rock knowing, Claire said. Make the most of it while we're on holiday.

I don't know, said Annie. I'm not normally into that.

By ten, the bar was beginning to get busy. Middle-aged men with shaved heads and short torsos sauntered across the floor towards the girls' booth.

You can tell the barmaids are all foreign birds because of the way they dress, a legal clerk explained to Nikki thickly.

You can tell they're foreign because of their hair, said his friend.

I can tell you're all crapauds because of your pin dicks, Claire said. Rudeness only encouraged the men here, who cheered and bought the girls a round.

And I can tell you're from Guernsey because you're all slags, one of them said, tossing back tequila with salted fingers, his candy-striped tie hanging loose around his collar. But the girls knew what they wanted from this early crowd of building site managers and estate agents, and it was free drinks only. They laughed harder at the men's jokes and drank everything that was pushed their way.

Men in shiny suits and shoes big as boats were filing in now. Bankers, lawyers, tax consultants and analysts. Men in their twenties who lived in new-build sea-view apartments, men in their thirties who bought upmarket supermarket DINE IN FOR TWO FOR £10 deals for weekend girlfriends. Their eyes rolled around the room like schoolboys' marbles, looking for likely fucks.

You could get with that one, he's all right. Claire pointed out an accountant to Annie, who was ripping at her straightened split ends. He's got a decent job so his flat's probably nice enough to go back to. Bet he's got a power shower.

Do you think he's nice?

He's got a wedding ring on, Becky said, divvying up a bottle of wine into four glasses.

You see. All the good ones have gone, Annie said.

Count yourself lucky, Nikki said, starting to cry. You don't have to get married.

Once her tears started, Nikki was unruly. She wasn't sure whether Marc was The One, or whether there was such a thing at all. She was certain that she didn't like the erratic hours that Marc kept as a paramedic, or the cannabis he smoked to keep his sleep in check. For the past three months, Nikki had been starving herself to fit into her fishtail wedding dress, and the alcohol was getting to her more quickly than the others. She didn't mean to get so upset, she whined, saying that she was sorry over and over again.

Nikki was crying and Annie had the gummy look of someone who was about to, whether out of sympathy or discomfort, Claire wasn't sure; Annie could be like that. Meanwhile Becky intoned her relationship advice with even more condescension than she had done when she was sober. Marriage was about compromise, Becky slurred, and romance not worth bothering with. There was no such thing as love, only reasonable and balanced decisions about how to manage a household and raise children.

Do you really not believe in love? Annie wailed.

Claire was feeling comparatively sober, whatever the concertina of bar receipts bulking up her purse might say to the contrary. She was well versed in hiding her capacity for drinking, had learned over the past ten years to increase her measures and offer to buy more rounds. At times like this, she wished she had a lower tolerance. A blackout would be heavenly: she missed their sudden ease. So she went to the bar to get some napkins and a pint of tap water to perk up the bride-to-be, and ordered another shot for herself. It was only eleven thirty. There were hours to drain away before they could reasonably go back to the hotel.

Let me get that for you, the man next to her said.

She twisted around in the crowd to look at her paying neighbour. He was good-looking, sweating only as much as the rest.

Can you add a double vodka lemonade and lime to that too then, please, Claire said to the barmaid.

And the shot? the barmaid quizzed.

Yes, and the shot, she said. Claire could feel the alcohol

perfuming her bra. A vein was pricking her left eyelid so that she had to squint against the lighting. Go on, what's your name then?

I'm Harry, said Harry, a thirty-something city boy on an island without a city. He drank Jim Beam like it was Talisker and stood with his legs wide apart.

I'm Claire, said Claire.

Tell me something about yourself, Claire, Harry said. I'd like to get better acquainted.

My sister killed herself three months ago, Claire said. She knew from past experience that men like this didn't listen anyway. That wasn't why he was interested in talking to her.

Oh dear, that's terrible, he said in her ear. Harry wrested his arm around Claire's bare shoulders and handed over his credit card. Claire thanked him with a sticky-eyed smile, and the barmaid returned the credit card with her eyes already rolling over the next customer. Harry watched Claire down her shot and then handed her the double vodka, as you might give a child a drink of water to take away the taste of the medicine. Talk to me, he said.

She took an overdose, she said, letting Harry lead her over to a corner sofa. The ice chinked against his very white teeth as he drained his whiskey and Coke. The music was vertiginously loud. It wasn't the first time she'd tried doing it, she said. I didn't really take it seriously at first. I didn't get on with her much.

Harry opened his mouth wide at that point as if to say something. Claire waited, and the song that was playing finished, but still he didn't say anything. His cheeks were flushed from the drink and the talk. So she laughed. Then Harry laughed, and he covered her lips with his. His tongue was fat, muscular, pointed at the tip. She had the sensation of being open for dipping, like a disposable paper cup of garlic mayo on the side of takeaway chips. Claire had never cheated on Brian before. God knows her colleagues had tried their hardest to encourage her: heavying their hands on her knees, under hems, on the small of her back, their fingertips brushing against her nipples when they handed her palm-warmed wine glasses.

Brian, on the other hand, had always treated their marriage much as he had done their non-stick Teflon pans: with little respect. It had been an insoluble argument between Claire and her older sister, each adamant that the other's partner wasn't good enough for them. They had never much liked each other's boyfriends, even as teenagers, but the men they finally married were kindling to their rows. Kat said that Claire's Brian was a limpet, clinging on to what he could at any given opportunity; whereas Claire couldn't stand Kat's partner for never helping her look after his son. Kat's truths were often cruel because she was usually right, so Claire hated their spats and the humiliation they wrought. You can love people too much, Kat had screamed the last time Claire had shut her sister's front door. But Claire wished that she'd listened to her sister's raw advice now. She could feel Harry's tongue dart into her ear and his fingers fumble at the unrelenting grip of her underwire.

Claire wished she'd kicked Brian out of their house when she first found out he'd been to bed with Becky. She should have changed the locks and asked Kat to move in, two sisters together. She should have told Becky when she'd discovered her text messages, written proof of those sidelong glances and rippling laughs at group get-togethers. Flirting may as well be flag-waving, anyone with eyes could see it. There was no subtlety to affairs, only rushed sex and unprecedented showering. The gas bill had gone up with all the extra hot water. She had been collecting evidence to confront them with for so long that it now felt petty to bring up kilowatts and pence: it made Claire feel even more humiliated. Claire wasn't sure when exactly her best friend had first fucked her husband but by the time her sister's suicide came, it all fell out of focus.

The first overdose didn't work, Claire said to Harry as he snuffled over her neck. His fingers were now hooked under the knackered elastic of her black knickers. Claire couldn't see the other girls. She could taste her tears salty on Harry's tongue and she had to pull away to breathe. He wasn't listening. She could talk, not talk: he wasn't listening. The room was sliding away from her now, the sambuca and vodka and rosé roiling beneath the tightness of her dress.

Everyone said she was doing it for attention but she tried again and then again before they sent her to the Castel Hospital, said Claire. When she got out, nobody would invite her out, nobody wanted to see her. Our mum didn't want to see her, didn't want anybody to hear about what was happening. Even Kat felt she was embarrassing us all. Social services didn't want her to see her little boy as Ric said she wasn't to be trusted alone with him and the police were called to the flat a bunch of times. She wasn't dangerous, I don't think. Just unhappy. I hadn't spoken to her for three weeks when she finally managed to do it, we'd had a row because she found out I'd given her husband money to help with the childcare. I said I was only trying to help.

Claire paused and Harry pushed his fourth finger inside

her, sucking her tit through the fabric of her dress. The slinky fabric of Harry's suit slithered over her thighs as he used his knee to wedge open her legs further. She took another overdose, said Claire, adding, there were only ten of us at the funeral. She reached over to down the remainder of her drink before letting him carry on all over her, her hands clasped around his sweat-wetted neck and eyes stinging with wilted mascara.

It was difficult to talk about her sister to the girls; none of them really knew what to say. Claire knew that they hadn't liked Kat anyway, not at school, not after. Nikki had accompanied Claire to the funeral, had put on her best dark dress even, but to Claire, the awkwardness was almost as bad as the ragged grief. Annie had said she was sorry but she hadn't known Kat at all. Becky didn't offer to attend the service and had instead sent a bouquet of freesias, which Brian later insisted that Claire write a thank-you note for. This remark only signalled to Claire that the affair was in full heat by then. All those afternoons spent at the bank discussing funeral finance: the practical arrangements of grief had opened up plenty of opportunities for illicit quickies. Claire had taken one week's compassionate leave off work, in which she'd black-bagged Kat's clothes for the charity shop and made tea for Kat's husband when really she'd needed it herself, then returned to the office as if nothing had changed.

You need to give yourself time, Brian had said. You need to think about yourself, have some space, do whatever you need.

On her first Friday night out after the funeral, Claire had cadged shots off colleagues she barely knew and was put in a taxi home by nine. Brian put her to bed with a pint of water and a washing-up bowl. You need to start looking after yourself, Brian had said, tying her hair away from her wet face as she threw up everything inside of her. You're not your sister. Claire had wiped her mouth, her stomach empty except for the anger.

She did begin to feel calmer but it took too long for Brian. He began to needle her for her forced sense of fun, for crying in taxis home, for not doing the housework, for her string of excuses not to have sex with him. It was remarkable how little self-awareness he had. Well she was having sex now, Claire thought. She would if she had to.

Claire ground herself into the financial analyst's hands with such decisiveness that he squealed with surprise. She bit his bottom lip, the tang of iron in their mouths, and led him to the swing door of the female toilets. She felt seventeen again, the transactional urgency was so familiar. One of the women from behind the bar was cleaning the only available cubicle, the other was Sellotaped shut with a number of 'out of order' notices on its door like a crime scene. Claire and Harry kissed wetly by the sinks while the worker mopped the floor, sloshed bleach and caustic soda around the grime-grouted tiles, refilled the toilet paper units. The sanitary waste bin she left well alone. She took her time restocking the condoms and non-applicator tampons in the pound machine, keeping her eyes tacked on Claire and her exposed bra at all times. Claire could still feel the judgement of the woman's gaze even once the empty cubicle door was banged shut and locked. She couldn't shake the hard stare from her mind even once her dress was pushed well up above the knives of her hips and her heels were clattering either side of Harry's shirted back. The strap of her handbag kept slipping off her shoulder so she had to keep hitching it up while he pushed again, again, again. He moaned a lot. She was too drunk to feel much but she didn't care, clinging on tight to his neck in case he dropped her. She had hoped it would be over quicker than this.

JO LE POIDEVIN IS A WHORE, the graffiti on the door opposite read. The writing zig-zagged over every surface in sight. SEXY GIRLS IN YOUR AREA was stickered at intervals, printed in batch on the kind of rectangular white office labels that Claire used for mail merges at work. There were also big cartoonish hearts scrawled in biro, and smiley faces, sad faces. The more Claire read, the more she saw, like spotting an ant on the pavement. MARIE EATS DICKS, someone had scrawled. CALL LAYLA FOR ANAL. Bitches, cows, sluts, slags, cumbags. Ugly, fat, thick. The shame and spite of it all. Claire read the comments until Harry finished with a grunt. He handed her some toilet roll to wipe between her legs and she felt her insides retracting.

You go first, she said to him, dodging his beery kiss. Better go out separately so we're not seen together.

He obeyed, apparently relieved to be out of the confined, chemical-stinking space now that there was no reason to talk to each other any more. He left her alone by the sinks with a goodbye in the form of a too-hard pinch on the arse. The door closed against the pumping music beyond. She caught her breath. Claire smoothed out the rumples from her clothes and reached for the zip-up make-up pouch inside her hand-bag. She reapplied two coats of mascara, slid lip gloss over her lips. Wiped away the eyeliner that had clawed around her sockets from all the crying. She took out her kohl pencil to reapply it but paused at the insults shouting backwards at her reflection.

BECKY FUCKS BOYFRIENDS, she could have written. Or BECKY IS A LIAR. She imagined Becky's face on seeing her lies outlined for the women of Jersey to see. Would she well up or throw up, Claire wondered, or would she not even recognise herself in the comments? Claire tried to think of something she could write that would punish her friend. But the anger and doubt, all those mealy months of it: Claire couldn't bring herself to care any more. She pushed the kohl pencil to the wall and scrawled in large, looping letters: I LOVE MY SISTER.

Back in the bar, Claire ordered a glass of tap water and a cranberry juice, no vodka. The server was the same young woman who had been cleaning the toilets. She didn't smile at Claire or say thank you, not even when she tipped her with a five-pound note. The server just shook her head. Claire returned to the girls, who had regrouped on the dancefloor and were skittering to the music like newborn colts.

I've got to marry him, Nikki was saying above the tweaking pop. Her top gaped open on one side like a grin from where one of the bra fillers had fallen out.

Because he's the one, Annie nodded. You do love him really.

I want it to be my big day, Nikki said.

You were gone a long time, Becky said as she gulped her drink.

Becky set the clammy glass down on a podium table and looked Claire up and down. There was a thoroughness to Becky's inspection, which Claire imagined had developed from her own recent need to carefully cover up love bites and bruises. Not that Brian ever looked at Claire any more: since the discovery of his affair and her sister's death, she'd gone down two dress sizes and a bra size, and he had never once made a comment. But women had a knack for noticing things. Becky wiped her hands on her leather-look skirt, waiting for an answer.

Claire chewed up the insides of her cheeks while she tried to work out her alibi, her tongue thickening from all the drink. Had Becky seen her go to the loos with the guy? Would she tell Brian? How much would a divorce cost and how long would it take to sort out the flat? Everyone at work would be asking about it. The ending was in motion now. Claire was starting to feel dizzy. She could smell tart body odour on the nylon of her dress. The paralysis in her jaw was worse than when she and Becky had tried ketamine in Candie Gardens when they were fourteen. Perhaps she had had too much to drink after all, she couldn't catch the right words.

You are okay, aren't you? Becky said. She took Claire's hand and pulled her further into the mince of dancing drunks. I didn't know where you went and you weren't answering your phone. I was worried about you.

You were worried about me, Claire repeated. The music was wheeling and Claire was finding it hard to distinguish her feet from everyone else's. She felt Becky's fingers smear away the smudges of make-up from her eyes, lips, eyebrows. She resented the female capacity for tears. She closed her eyes as Becky steadied her.

You can have him, said Claire. I don't want him.

You what, Becky said. She didn't say anything else.

I don't want him, Claire said again.

I don't get it, Becky said, making a face like she'd just had a gin shot.

Claire left Becky boggling and moved further into the crowd to dance beside Nikki. She pretended she was too drunk to speak for the rest of the night, although in reality it was because she had said everything now. She could see the glow of Becky's phone as she tried to type a message. Claire checked her own phone and blinked through her clumped eyelashes at the single text from Brian asking if she was having the weekend of her life. She didn't reply. She continued to dance with Nikki and Annie until the house lights flipped on. She kissed them both on the cheeks, saying how glad she was that they were both there. She changed into foldaway flat shoes for the walk back to the hotel, pulling their soft elasticated heels up over her ballooning blisters.

They slept two to a bed in their hotel room that night, as Becky had insisted on keeping hen costs down as much as they could. Claire lay still on her side, the hangover already strobing through her blood, her ribcage an armour against her hot organs sprawling out over the thin, bobbled bed-clothes. The curtains didn't meet in the middle and the light streamed through the pink of her closed eyelids.

Guilt and anger were pluming in her belly. She should've known she'd never get any acknowledgement from Becky: Becky never admitted anything. When they were growing up, Claire had had to hear about Becky's exploits from other people at school: how she'd stripped off in front of a whole house party of strangers to go swimming, or kissed a barman in Follies for a free round of Archers. Claire had always accepted both the lies and the fact she'd been lied to because she'd imagined that Becky knew that this was a tacit arrangement between them. I know that you know, one of their old secrets. But as she lay next to her old friend on the shabby bedsheets, she thought how Becky had probably taken her for a mug all along. Nobody'll stand up for you if you don't stand up for yourself, Kat used to say when Claire would be snivelling over something that Becky had done or said. Just you wait and see, if you don't believe me.

Becky rolled over in her sleep, her dribble dampening the pillow, and stretched her arm around Claire. Was this what she did in bed with Brian? Claire thought, lifting her friend's heavy limb back to her half of the bed. Becky's arm slowly returned to embrace her. Claire left the arm in place that time, breathing shallowly under the unexpected weight of it, and woke in the morning to find that she was holding Becky's hand as she had once held her sister's. Even though she was awake, Claire kept her eyes shut a little longer. She could hear the thrum of a bin lorry waiting in the street, the rattle of recycling and refuse being slung into it. She opened her eyes to see the last of the streetlights being switched off and the ready morning blank behind them.

Just you wait.

Real Nice

Fort George, 2018

Luc has been parked up for forty minutes now. He would rather be listening to hip-hop but it's better to have Radio 4 playing just in case anyone walking by becomes suspicious. He checks the screen on an unregistered mobile phone but there have been no new messages or calls since the morning, so he replaces it in the driver's door compartment alongside the tattered old Guernsey A–Z map and a small flick-knife. Carly has put him in touch with a friend of hers and he should be here any minute. He's had his lunch already so he's not in a rush, and the respectability of Fort George and its expensive candy-coloured villas lends an ease to the transaction. He watches a gardener prune a bare pear tree, and the magpie that is preening itself amidst its branches. Hydrangea and camellia shrubs bustle in the breeze. It is almost peaceful.

Luc does different stints in different parts of the island on different days. He dresses for each occasion accordingly, today in a checked navy suit and pale blue shirt without a tie. Often businessmen from the offshore banks and insurance firms will drop by on a lunch break for a pick-me-up, ready with machine-crisped cash in manila envelopes. Some of these clients, Luc now knows very well: he sees them here and about the other wealthy suburbs at Fort George, sees them in the town's few nightclubs on a Wednesday and a Friday, raising a beer to them across the hammering dancefloor. One of the younger guys bought him a souvlaki when they bumped into each other down the takeaway joint by the bus stop last week, the night already draining away. These men tend to be his best customers. They pay, they want no fuss.

As well as the offshore bankers on short-term visas, Luc has learned that there are many types of rich people. There are the ready-made rich, the older moneyed wives who walk down the prim paths from their oversized mansions towards his car, well-groomed and well-educated and decked in cream bouclé blazers and patent loafers. There are the championship racing drivers, and their bored girlfriends. There are reclusive artists and one-time musicians. There are a lot of lawyers. Proportionally, very few people on the island are rich but, fortunately for Luc, those with wealth only have a handful of options for how to spend it. At Christmas and Easter and over July and August, Luc also receives calls from a number of wealthy students back on their holidays from redbrick universities, desperate to speed up their time at home. Luc tries not to deal with kids younger than that, steers clear of the schools and surfer meet-ups. He doesn't use children, remembering how he hadn't even begun to use deodorant when he started grafting. Besides, Luc doesn't need any more aggravating factors, if the shit were to ever hit the fan. But it hasn't for a long time, not badly, and not just because he's lucky: because he's got the hang of this.

There is a knock on the smoked glass of the car window. Luc peers through, sees a suit, and loudly tells the guy to come in. He unlocks the car using the automatic button by the gearstick. The passenger door opens and a tall man folds himself into the seat, shutting the door along with the gush of noise outside behind him. The customer slips his jacket button undone as if he's at a work meeting. Then he puts on his seat belt and quickly fumbles again to unclip it, having realised that the car is stationary and Luc has not moved to switch the engine on. Luc tries not to smirk, not wanting to embarrass his customer; not when it's their first meeting, at least, although it can be a useful tactic to keep them in check. The black seat belt winds itself back across the man's solid chest with a gentle whirr and he looks up at Luc.

We've not met, Luc says. You're a friend of Carly's? She told you about me?

The man looks at him fully now, twisting round in his seat so that his torso and head is entirely facing Luc.

Fuck, the customer goes. This is fucking hilarious.

What?

Luc?

It's not hilarious, Luc thinks, looking at the man, but it is something. Luc feels the way he used to when the boys at school used to start fights in the pavilion after games, fearful and thrilled all at once. He's glad he has dressed up for Fort George today and not for the Bowl. He catches sight of himself in the rear-view mirror. He looks good, he thinks, he looks like the older version of himself that he'd hoped he might turn into.

Gavin, he says. Carly didn't mention it was you. She doesn't tend to give out names.

Maybe she thought we wouldn't know each other, Gavin says, holding out his hand for Luc to shake.

Luc considers it. Then he takes it, something he rarely does now, saying, Why would you need a seat belt on, eh? We're not going spinning.

Yeah, right, Gavin says. He mimes an exaggeratedly embarrassed face, pulling his symmetrical features into a clownish grimace. It doesn't suit him.

Luc feels nervous looking directly at Gavin so he looks at Gavin's hands instead, which have neat short nails and are folded in his lap like a napkin. Luc wonders if he eats out much, which are his favourite restaurants on the island. Maybe he cooks at home too, perhaps he buys proper books and follows the recipes, running his index finger along the list of speciality ingredients. Luc didn't spend much time at home when he was younger and has never found the time to learn to cook. He has his own place now, though, nicely lit in the evenings, a balcony, rainfall shower, big telly. He imagines showing Gavin around. This is the master, the en suite.

So. Carly said you could fix me up, Gavin says with a nod.

Yeah, Luc says. Sure.

Funny, isn't it? Gavin says.

Yeah.

She'll laugh her head off when she hears.

Will she?

Oh, she'll absolutely wet herself, Gavin says.

Luc thinks that he has seen Carly wet herself before but not because she was laughing. Carly's one of his regulars, a stringy thirty-something with furred arms and very white teeth. Her eyes are big and ultramarine blue, so sometimes it looks as if she's crying when really she's just high. She calls Luc from a new number most weeks, having littered her possessions around the island's high-end bars and nightclubs. He doesn't know what she does for work but he imagines that she ferrets her chemical energy into something impressive. She probably meets all her targets, motivates her team. He doesn't know how she knows Gavin. Carly is a good customer but not, Luc thinks, a happy one.

We were good mates, weren't we?

Good mates? Luc repeats.

We used to go crabbing, Gavin says.

Luc is surprised to find he can't remember this. He has a good memory for most childhood things. His cousin Eva always ribs him for remembering insignificant details about their grandmother's house, knowing exactly where in the attic she'd hidden the T-shirt signed by the Beatles on their island visit in 1963. He could tell you the locker combinations for a dozen of his sixth-form classmates, which ones had the most pocket money and the sandwiches worth stealing. He can remember a lot of the times that he spent with Gavin Mauger, but he can't remember going crabbing with him, not once. He remembers the beaches that they went to together: Port Soif with its sickle of sand, Petit Port with its two hundred and seventy steps that felt like a secret the further you went down. Moulin Huet with its shady lanes that could take you into darkness even in the daytime. Soldiers Bay too. They got high and got each other off. It was dizzying, deafening. Luc had felt invincible: it didn't matter if they got caught, which they did, sometimes. Once, Luc had had the vague hope that they would both be arrested at the same time, whether for dealing or indecency or underage sex it didn't matter, so that they might spend the rest of their years together, inseparable and full of spite for the world outside.

Sometimes we went jumping down by Jerbourg, Gavin adds. Can you imagine doing that now? It was so stupid, when I think about it. Literally jumping off a cliff. Off a fucking massive cliff into the sea, like, really? It's a death wish. It's a miracle none of us got brain damage or lost a limb. When I tell people about growing up in Guernsey, honestly, people think we're all mad.

We were just really young, Luc says.

Thank God there wasn't social media then is all I'm saying.

How do you mean?

If people could see us now how we were then.

Right.

It'd be so embarrassing.

Well you've turned out all right, anyway.

How do you mean?

Nice suit, Luc says.

Thanks.

Posh.

Boring old uniform, really, Gavin says. It's not like they force you to wear one but it's sort of a given.

Like they'll give you detention if you don't, says Luc.

That's exactly it. Gavin starts laughing.

Remember when we spent a whole week on our own in Mr Martel's office?

What? Gavin is still laughing. No, we didn't.

We did something to that Ozanne kid so he made us do every single lesson with him, so he could keep an eye on us. It was mental.

I don't think that was me, mate.

You don't remember the Ozanne kid?

Gavin shrugs and shakes his head. Must have been one of your things, he says.

My things?

When you used to go apeshit, he says. You used to fly off the handle at anything. What a joker. What was the song you always used to sing?

I don't know, says Luc.

There was a rap you did.

I really don't know, says Luc. He can remember how the two of them sat, a few feet apart, on either side of the head-teacher's desk. Sunlight slicing through the metal blinds. Mr Martel hadn't even risked turning his back on them to answer the door. It's your future, he'd told them both, removing the scissors and compasses and protractors from their pencil cases.

Luc looks at Gavin in his fitted suit, his shirt cuffs knotted with small twists of silvery yarn, and his softly coiffed hair that's the pale blond colour of oven chips. He smells good. His shave is close-cut in a reassuring way, unlike the reddish chapped skin that's flaking under Luc's own stubble. Gavin looks like a genuine businessman. Luc starts to feels like he has been tricked, somehow, that he has come to a party in fancy dress when Gavin and everyone else has turned up in their own clothes.

Can you believe they just pay me to sell money? Gavin says.

Not really, Luc says.

He wants to say that Gavin was shit at school, that he hated maths and didn't do his homework. I was always the smart one, Luc wants to say, how do you think I'm doing this? Luc thought nothing of it when Gavin went off to university with half of their sixth-form class. He knew that everyone who leaves the island comes back at some point. The island has a pull on its people like the moon on the tide. Luc certainly never expected to feel as if he was being left behind.

People used to assume he was doltish when he was first starting out. Clients talked to him slowly. At first he thought it was because they were watching their words out of fear but he soon realised it was because they thought he couldn't keep up. One or two tried to cheat him. Fuck this, he thought to himself one Thursday, pulping a customer's face against a corrugated garage door with his fists. How can respect be so hard for people to find?

It's all right actually, Gavin says. The guys in the office are a laugh. I don't mind the hours either, it's not like there's much else I'd be doing. I was told that investment would be all work hard, play hard, but to be honest, it's all play when it's other people's money. What's to worry about, you know? It all comes around.

Sounds good, Luc says.

Yeah, yeah. I love the lifestyle, if I'm honest, but the time will come.

For what? Luc says after a short pause that Gavin does nothing to fill.

The girlfriend wants to settle down, Gavin replies. I said let's give it a couple more years in London, eating out, holidays, what have you, then we can go back to base camp and get married. Free childcare. It's too easy not to. We can have a house here for the cost of our flat in London, it's so cheap.

It's not that cheap, Luc thinks at first, and then he hears

again in his mind what Gavin has really said. He is planning
to get married in the future, he is going to try for children.
Luc tries to think of something to say in response that is
less shocked than his immediate reaction, so he asks, Your
girlfriend's from Guernsey too?

Yeah, I don't think you'd know her, Gavin says. She was
a few years above us at school, although weirdly we didn't
meet till we were both in London. We met at a Liberation
Day thing in Holloway. It's funny how when you go to the
mainland, you meet all these little Guerns and crapauds
popping up everywhere like Hungry Hippos. Isn't that mad?

Sounds mad.

We both hate London as much as the rock, to be honest,
but it sort of meant we bonded. Isn't it strange how it ends
up? I'm back for a couple of months on secondment, doing
a trial run to see if we could hack it later on.

What's her name?

Oh, you really wouldn't know her.

Luc can't believe that there would have been a single
person at their school who he hadn't known. He was sure
that he knew everyone, that everyone knew him, give a
good five years either side of his age. He thinks of all the
girls who'd been in sixth form, and tries to picture who
stayed on the island and who left as soon as they could. The
thought process is hard work and there are blanks where
faces should be. He can't visualise Gavin with a wife, a kid,
a semi-detached house.

Sounds like everything's working out then, says Luc.

Most of the time, I'd say so, goes Gavin. But then, sometimes it gets you. A lot of us our age are feeling like that,
though, aren't we? What are we all doing in offices, sitting

around, looking at things? What's the point, you know? What's the fucking point? What about you?

Oh, I don't work in an office, Luc laughs. He is looking at the jagged edges of his thumbnails where he has chewed and ripped at them. There is the pale pink silk of skin left from where a recent scab has fallen off his left knuckle.

No, but. What do you do?

What do I do? Luc thinks. He earns good money nowadays and he tries to have a good time doing it. He doesn't grub around. He talks to all sorts of people in the way that a doctor might, or a teacher or a cab driver perhaps. He isn't fussy, so long as they pay. He could tell you what is happening in the Court, who will be up in front of the Magistrate for what and which police officers will be pushing what case. He knows which bands are the ones worth seeing at the Vale Earth Fair, which school is going to the dogs, who will be standing in the next election and which of the award-winning restaurants have mice. He takes care that his customers do not feel intimidated by him, that they are happy to have a chat and confide in him: they will keep coming back to him that way.

The patter keeps him company too, not that he is especially lonely. Luc can find company when he wants it. He has met the eyes of men in the mirrors of Michelin-starred restaurants while their wives and colleagues are waiting for coffees at their table. Every few months, he likes to leave a nightclub with the stares of the podium dancers and binge drinkers on him and his chosen conquest. Sometimes he doesn't even have to offer out his stash to them, although he is happy to share what he's got when the mood takes him. He took one guy to St Malo last year, where they ate moules at a bistro beneath the ramparts. Luc had liked it when he said thank you.

I do this, Luc says with a smile. He means it to sound light, flippant even, but he senses his tone is too contrived because Gavin is now shifting around in the car seat in his shiny suit. Luc hides his knuckles, which suddenly feel huge and heavy.

I guess I thought it was just a phase, Gavin says with a softness that sounds like pity. I thought you'd grow out of it.

A sense of humiliation burbles up inside Luc that he has to snap back at, saying, Well, I thought you were here to buy coke.

Gavin turns away. He looks out of the window to where the gardener is strimming a high hedge in the front garden of one of the mansions, leaves falling down around him like wedding confetti. The radio programme twitters through the silence, discussing the originality of a theatre show in London that Luc knows he will never see. Luc wishes that Gavin would say sorry and they could laugh about it. Maybe they could even do a line together. They could go to one of the bars afterwards and have a drink, Luc could buy champagne and insist on paying for it.

Gavin reaches inside his jacket pocket for his wallet, frowns, then pats down his trousers and retrieves it from the left-leg pocket. It's plump, the leather worn and lustrous. While he thumbs through the blue and brown ten-pound notes, not counting out loud, Luc tries to think what he could say to transform the conversation into the one he'd long wanted. Except it's like Gavin hasn't rehearsed his lines right and Luc can't pick up his cue. So Luc continues to watch him, the words out of reach.

Here's sixty, Gavin says. That's right, isn't it? That's what Carly said.

Gavin unclips two twenty-pound notes and two tens. They are smooth, as if he has been to the cashpoint specifically to withdraw the sum earlier this morning. He passes Luc the cash with his fingers on one corner of the notes, so that he doesn't have to touch Luc's hands.

We don't normally do it but we're having a gathering, Gavin goes on. People will expect to have the option. Just trying to make friends, I guess. It's been a long time since we both lived here properly.

I don't need to know, Luc says.

I just don't want you to think that we're those kind of people, Gavin follows.

Luc nods as if Gavin is right in his assessment that there exist those kind of people. Luc has heard this talk before, although normally from someone older who has had little contact with real people going about their everyday lives – having fun, having bad days, having parties. Gavin used to be one of them, he was sure. Now he has deliberately removed himself from the rest of us, Luc thinks, and he has the money to do so. It's remarkable, what can be bought.

Do you need instructions with it too? Luc says.

He pushes Gavin's money into his trouser pocket, feeling it crumple as he crams it further down the leg. The rest of the day's takings is folded with care and clipped together tidily inside Luc's suit jacket. Normally he takes great pride in flamboyantly adding more money to the wodge in front of clients, untying and retying the elastic band around the notes, reinforcing to new customers how everyone comes to him with their needs. How successful he is, how he excels at dealing. Now, he just wants it out of sight.

Gavin says nothing. His mouth is twisted slightly like he is chewing the inside of his cheeks. His hands are placed in his lap again, scooping one thumbnail under the other as if there is dirt beneath it. Luc can't be sure if these gestures are the same ones that he used to make when he was worrying about getting caught by the police or their parents. He had definitely done something like that with his hands the time they'd got cautioned for beating up that kid so badly at the Liberation Day fair, or when they had the Vazon kiosk toilets evacuated for bagging. He always thought Gavin used to wrinkle his right eye in a wince when someone shouted at him. Maybe Luc just saw someone do that in a film once.

Luc leans back in his seat, reaches his arm around behind him, and flicks open the small leatherette compartment on the other side of the gearstick. He takes out a Jiffy bag. He pushes over the inner bubble-wrap lining to reveal a thin windowpane envelope tucked inside, out of which he takes one small clear baggy of white powder. He looks Gavin in the embarrassed pink gloss of his face as he hands him the cocaine. Then he folds over the envelope again, tucks it back in place inside the larger envelope, replaces it in the compartment and taps the lid shut.

Gavin slips the slim baggy inside his jacket. His hand is on the door release already, his teeth still working over the hot inner flesh of his cheeks. There is no time now for Luc to say anything he hasn't said. The deal is done. He is a dealer after all.

Enjoy yourself, Luc says. I hope your new friends like it.

Yeah, Gavin says. He opens the door and steps out, no thanks given, lowering his head.

Tell your friends they can get their orders through Carly, if they want more. No need to come to me direct, Luc says. Being this rude could lose him a customer, Luc knows, and he doesn't feel better for it either, exactly. But it has stopped him wondering, and waiting.

Fine by me.

Gav, he adds. They look at each other, the moment lengthens. Don't say you don't remember what we did to Nick Ozanne. I bet he hasn't forgotten you were there.

Gavin slams the car door.

Luc watches Gavin as he struts forward along the pavement, turns his head slightly back to check that nobody has seen him get out of the car, and then walks on at a brisk pace. He does up the middle button on his suit jacket and rounds the corner, out of sight.

Luc checks the time. He has another drop-off to make up at The Bridge at half past two. As he pulls out of the luxury estate and waits at the roundabout, he thinks how you can feel homesick for a time as much as a place.

The Lure

Canary Wharf, 2019

The seagulls were squabbling over something in
Montgomery Square. They were too far down for Josie
to see what exactly, and she couldn't hear their cries from
behind the reinforced glass, but she could make out a cluster
of small white bodies whirling around the concrete like sea
scum. Everything from the world outside was silenced behind
the windows, from the grungy barges pushing on up the
Thames to the black cabs crawling towards the underground
car parks. It looked sunny out today – thirty-two degrees
from what she'd read on her morning trawl of the internet,
comparing one news site to another, checking the weather
in all of the cities that she could think of. It had been hot
all week, the pavements steaming and the parks browning,
and the weather was predicted to continue through to next
Tuesday at least. It was hard to tell the temperature when the
office itself was so vigorously air-conditioned. She watched
the seagulls for a while longer. She'd read that more and more

of them were moving from the sea to urban spaces because of the food scraps they could find inland. One of the gulls wrenched something from the beak of another and flew away at speed into the glare of the sky above. The windows of the office blocks opposite hers shone blue and purple, mirroring each other across Canary Wharf so that it looked as if the glossy towers filled the whole city.

Joanie?

Josie, she said. She drew up her smile.

Have you seen the latest statements? I can't find them and I can't find the trainee either.

No, Josie said. She paused before adding, But I can have a look.

That'd be great.

Great, she thought to herself in a voice caustic with can-do attitude, it's not my job but why not. She trotted towards the photocopier room, her heels sticking slightly in the thin ridges of the carpet floor-tiles on her way. It was a relief to be out of the refrigerated main office, and in a room with solid walls rather than see-through glass. She technically shared a private office with a senior associate but even when the door was shut, everything they did could be viewed by anyone walking past. Josie had recently requested an anti-glare screen.

Cardboard boxes of bundles and loose sheafs of A4 were stacked systematically on the floor, some marked with hand-written Post-its and others with the laminated labels of the reprographics department. She found the files she needed and flicked through the pages to see that the trainee hadn't done the work. She hated telling people off; it made her feel mean and ridiculous. She sorted out the different papers ready to feed into the photocopier. It wouldn't take long. She slotted in the first batch of pages and the machine hummed into action, the light strobing from under the lid. She upped the number of copies and the machine chirped on with its chore, churning out one duplicate after another. She took her phone out of her pocket. She had received three messages, two from her friend Chloe and one from her brother.

SO EXCITING YOU SHAGGER xxxxxxxxxxxx, Chloe said in her first message, the text punctuated with a series of graphic icons that included party poppers and a cat covering its eyes with yellow paws. The next message read: Have you seen him yet?

No, Josie hadn't seen him, but she wasn't worried. She actually felt excited: her friend's message conveyed everything that Josie felt about the night before. Josie had liked Tom for such a long time, since the very start of law school. She had liked him so much that she'd felt sure for years that something would have to happen, in spite of the warnings from her girl-friends that she shouldn't get her hopes up, and finally it had. Sex had never felt so much like an I told you so.

Tom was the kind of man whose hand women scanned to see if he was already wearing a wedding ring. He was a catch. He had the straight posture of someone who'd been in the cadet corps at a private school. Josie tried to imagine what it would have been like to have met Tom when they were younger but couldn't picture their teenage selves exist-ing in the same world. But it didn't matter how they had got together, she told herself, because the fact was that they now had. Yeah, so she and Tom had been blind drunk the night before but that was the only way that things ever happened between people in this city, whether you were twenty-two or thirty-two; that's how Josie had explained it to her flatmate over microwaved porridge in the kitchen that morning. They had been friends for such a long time that these things didn't happen by accident.

She hadn't seen Tom yet today, or spoken to him. He worked on the floor above. She wasn't sure whether he would have told any of their friends yet, and she began to worry that she shouldn't have even told Chloe. Chloe had been telling her to start taking dating seriously, if she really wanted to meet someone decent at this age, and seemed overly invested in last night's developments. Josie didn't know how to reply to her so she closed the message and clicked to open the other one from her brother. See u at 1 yes xx, he said.

She pressed the button on the photocopier again for more copies and spotted a chip in her grey nail polish. She hoped that Tom hadn't noticed it, although perhaps it had happened during or even afterwards. She picked at the edge of the chipped area until the varnish peeled off in one fat strip. Then she eased it off the next nail, and the next. She could go to the nail bar after work and get another colour done, as she did most weeks. She thought about booking a bikini wax. She was glad she had shaved her legs at least. She considered messaging Tom, perhaps sending him a link to something over the office's internal chat system, maybe an article about the best pub menus in Camberwell or a meme from The Office, but Josie couldn't shy away from the traditional notion that he should get in touch with her first. After all, when she'd slunk into a cab at four o'clock that morning, eyes lambent with booze and oxytocin and the skin on her chin chapped scarlet, he had said he would speak to her later. When was later? And what would he say?

The photocopier light went off and she scooped up the warm paper from the copy tray. Josie separated out the requisite sheets and slipped them into order, hole punched them in thick blocks, and threaded them back into their box file. She yawned. Her thighs were a bit sore from all of last night's effort. She tried to remember the specific moves she'd made but couldn't. She reassured herself this was definitely because she had been fully in the moment and not because she had been hammered. She checked her phone again and replied to her brother, who was passing through the city for the day and had offered to meet her for lunch. She confirmed the time. She picked at a remaining fleck of nail varnish and switched the light off as she left the room.

Josie returned to her desk and laid out the box files in neat stacks. She opened up the internet and bought a pair of skinny jeans and a plum matte lipstick that she had seen featured in a free lifestyle magazine on the Tube. Josie had long spent a good one to two hours of her office day looking up things to buy, short courses to take, holidays to go on and even glasses to wear in case she ever needed them, and now she thought about what things would look good in her life beside Tom. Nine-carat yellow-gold hoop earrings with single pearl drops, cashmere-blend sweaters, sets of sunrise-coloured cast-iron pans. Training as a solicitor is a great way to use your brain, the marketers had told her when she signed up for the graduate scheme on the exhibition stand in her university's exam hall; but after nearly a decade of office work, she had developed the ability to live a whole other fantasy life in her mind. She had been wary of bringing Tom into this imagined realm before, but now something had happened, and it was happening. So she looked up some loafers with block heels that would look good with the new jeans, and tried to weigh up whether they would be too much to wear to a date at a pub. She wondered if they would make her feel like a rich person and not just someone spending money.

Over the past few months, Josie had also spent time online trying to find out whether her long-term ex was cheating on his new girlfriend. None of that mattered now things were starting with Tom. She pictured bumping into her ex with Tom on her arm, thought about what her ex would say and how she would smile with a shrug that said it couldn't be helped. She knew that Tom's family had a holiday home in Brittany and wondered if she might finally get to see it. She googled Brittany holiday homes and clicked her way through the many sun-slanted photos. There were so many options.

It was only ten past twelve. She looked up Tom's online profile on three different platforms, surveying his face from different angles. He had hidden a lot of his photos but then most people did now. She clicked back to the first website, where she surveyed their mutual friends' profiles. She scrolled through the profiles of people that she'd gone to law school with, and the people from university. She found a photo of Tom in his first year at Cambridge, under which a woman had commented with lots of hearts at the time. Josie clicked on to the woman's profile next and was pleased to see that her profile photo was one from her own wedding. They had a mutual friend: someone that Josie had been to school with on Guernsey. It looked like she'd moved back to the rock and was having a good time there, spending summers on the beaches and at barbecues, performing at the Sark Folk Festival and getting her kitchen redone. This was the lifestyle that many of her ex-schoolfriends now seemed to be enjoying, from what she could tell in their online photos. A few had had lavish weddings at beachfront hotels, their photos full of mauve blooms and wedding cakes whose edges were scraped almost bare of icing. Some had already had kids that were no longer babies, with more on the way. Josie hadn't kept in touch with any of them. She looked up Tom's profile again, looked at the straightness of his teeth and shoulders. Then she opened up her deleted items in her work inbox, and reread some of the recent email exchanges that they had sent to each other. It seemed unbelievable now that, this time yesterday, she had still doubted that he felt the same. She refreshed her inbox but he still hadn't messaged her.

At five to one, she put one heel in front of the other and marched past the rows of glass offices and the pool of central desks. Some of the staff were already eating in front of their computers, forking through chicken salads while they looked up airline deals. Josie didn't smile. She hadn't really made friends in this department. She got in the lift and smoothed her hair in its mirrored walls as it descended the building. She was tapping out of the staff turnstiles when she noticed Paul waiting for her in one of the swivel-chairs by the reception desk. He stood up as she skittered towards him, his arms outstretched.

You didn't have to come in here, I could've met you at the café, she said.

You didn't suggest one, he said. So I thought I'd find you, see what your work's like. Come here.

He pulled her into a hug and she could smell cigarettes on his breath. He had a scruff of unshaven hair around his jawline and greyed eyes that showed little sleep, but then he'd always had that look of the last person at the party. He was tanned and wrinkled, the island summer etched on his skin already. She never had got used to him looking older and knew that if she saw him more often, she wouldn't notice so much.

I wouldn't have recognised you with the hair, he joked, his fingers reaching for her brittle highlights. It's like you've been at the beach as much as me.

Fat chance, she said. I'm Vitamin D deficient.

Well, you've miraculously got taller.

Josie kicked out her legs so that her high heels flashed from beneath her trouser hems. She wiggled her patent leather toes at him.

Get you, Paul said. You can even walk in them.

You needn't sound so surprised.

You look great. I've missed you. How's your day going?

I expect you're starving, said Josie, leading him out of the cool reception into the glistering light of the square. The contrast was so searing that she had to put on her sunglasses. From behind the ochre lenses, she watched Paul look up and around him at the high-rise offices. Guernsey only had one tower block. It had eleven floors. She wondered if Paul thought this was like being in a film. She decided not to ask him.

They went to a popular café chain that Josie dropped by most days for breakfast or lunch or both, and Josie reached for the crayfish and avocado salad that she always bought. Paul stood by the ready-filled baguettes for a long while, inspecting the ingredients and the prices, picking up one item and putting it down. She stood apart from him while he chose. At the till, Josie insisted on paying for them both, picking them up a chocolate tiffin bar and a can of fizzy drink each. You're visiting town so that makes you my guest, she said, passing her credit card over to the server before Paul could hand over his cash.

The square outside was busy with suited and skirted workers having their sandwiches and wraps. The pair picked their way across the paving stones and up the steps towards a patch of shade beneath some fenced-off saplings. Josie spread her cardigan out on the ground and sat on it, stretching her legs straight out in front of her. The heat of the concrete thrummed beneath her. She pushed her heels off, her pop socks catching on the stone. Paul unwrapped his sandwich and butterflied the bread, picking out the raw tomatoes and putting them into the plastic packaging for the rubbish. Josie watched him as he then added in a layer of crisps, replaced the bread, and ate it.

They won't kill you, she said.

And how are you?

Fine, she said. Thank you. And you?

I'll need more detail, he said.

Work's fine. London's the same as last time. Big, expensive.

That's all right for you, he said. But you're enjoying it, though? Still?

It's fun. I'm having fun.

I'm guessing so, from the fact we never hear from you. Dad said he was going to try calling you last night, did you speak?

I was out.

Cool, he said. Good night?

Yeah, she said, covering the graze on her left arm with the salad box. Someone from work had a leaving do; we went out for a few drinks.

Well, Dad says hi, he said.

I did send him a birthday present.

What use has he got for a tie? He would've preferred a visit.

Flights are a rip-off in summer, you know that. Why fly to Guernsey when you could go to Rome for the same price?

You just spent fifteen quid on lunch, he said.

Josie speared a chunk of avocado with her plastic fork. She tried to think of something to say that was not about the night before with Tom and not about their father. She avoided his phone calls and emails with professional deftness. She did not want to hear his maudlin voice or shitty apologies. Paul had become his medium in the past few years, delivering his messages under proclaimed duress, and the added pressure was starting to strain their relationship too.

How's your course going? she asked. Paul had moved back home and was studying again, taking further education qualifications at the local college. He was going to be a landscape gardener, he had explained when he signed up, as there was enough business around the island. Plenty of big houses and people who didn't want to do the work themselves, and could afford not to. He'd get to be outdoors all day; he would be his own boss. He would make an absolute packet. Josie didn't know where he had got the money from to do the course in the first place, and didn't want to ask.

It's good, he said. I'll need to start my final project soon, so the field trip has been useful to get some ideas. We went around Kew; I've never seen anything like it. Bit different to Candie Gardens.

I still haven't been to Kew, she said. I keep meaning to.

All work and no play?

I do work hard actually, she said.

I'll let you off. Thanks for scheduling in a lunchtime appointment.

What time's your flight tonight?

Getting rid of me so soon, he laughed. I saw there were some shops by the station; I thought I might have a look around before I get the train back to Gatwick.

Stock up on T-shirts while you can.

You can get stuff delivered, you know, he said. There are such things as planes and ships. It's only an island, not a developing country. It's different now; it's easier to get what you want.

Did you know that when I first moved here, people used to ask if we had electricity at home? Josie said. They asked if we had schools. They said, do you have cars? How do you even get there? How come you speak English? Shouldn't you be French?

And these are your educated university friends, are they?

Talk about your friends, are they even out of prison yet?

Very funny.

Bet they're not, though.

Everyone's doing fine.

Even Tricky?

Even Tricky.

What's the big gossip, then? What's on the front page of the paper?

Nothing much, he said.

'Closed road now open'?

Fuck off.

You told me about that one years ago.

Stuff of legends.

Go on, tell me what's in the headlines, she said. What am I missing out on?

There's a lot of trouble with some big crabs moving down from the Russian coast because of the warmer waters. They're eating all of ours and the fish too. I caught one last week down by the Cup and Saucer. It was a giant fucker. Tasted great, though; we had it with spaghetti.

You made spaghetti?

Dad helped, said Paul. He's getting quite into cooking.

She shrugged and asked, Dad is doing okay, though?

He's really trying, he replied. He's in a programme now, goes every week. At the start, I used to sit in the car in the car park to make sure he went into the building and actually stayed there for the whole session. But I think now he really wants to get better. Mum leaving the island has been good, I reckon. It's sort of freed him, he doesn't have to worry he'll see her in the supermarket or in town and that. He can live his life.

You haven't heard from her?

Fuck no. Have you?

No.

Josie had seen their mum before she'd moved to London and her mum had moved to Southampton. They had gone for a coffee down at the tearooms at Moulin Huet, the lilac hydrangeas nodding in the breeze around the damp picnic table where they sat. Josie had felt that all of the couples and families around them could hear every word they were saying, and spoke so quietly that her mum snapped at her to speak up. Her mum had given her a torc necklace that Josie knew she'd never wear, and her eyes smarted from how misjudged it was. Don't get upset, her mum had said, you'll love London. Leaving here will be the best thing that'll happen to you. Why do you say that? Josie had said, holding the childish necklace with its silver seahorse charm between her fingers. Because you're just like me, her mum had said, you're always trying to be someone else. The words stayed with her no matter what Josie said, or did, or bought: they were a self-fulfilling prophecy. She hadn't told Paul about what her mum had said and hoped he couldn't see it for himself.

Reckon there are more seagulls here than back home, he said as a group of gulls strutted towards them with their beaks half-open. Do you remember when I used to teach you about all the different bird calls?

The what? she said. Across the blazing heat of the square, Josie could see Tom's suited figure striding out from the automatic double-doors of the office.

We used to sit in the lounge at Dad's, Paul carried on. We'd listen to all the birds, all the cormorants and razorbills and whatever, to see if we could guess which was which without looking. Remember how to tell if it's an oystercatcher?

I don't remember, she said, watching as Tom unknotted his tie and tucked it into the pocket of his jacket.

They sound like squeaky windscreen wipers, he laughed. You loved them the best.

Did I?

Yeah. I think of them whenever the car needs a service, he said.

Tom always seemed to be walking with such purpose, something she had felt in her stomach as he picked his way towards her through the bar the night before: there had been meaning in it. As Tom's figure approached, his features thrust into her eyeline, she noticed that he was walking over towards one of the upmarket chain restaurants on the other side of the square, and not in her direction. She pushed her sunglasses away from her face and into her hair, and sharply turned her head upwards as if she had seen a low-flying bird or an air ambulance. Tom saw her and waved, the desired effect. He ambled over.

I'm really proud of you, I know I should say it more, Paul was saying. I know it's not been easy for a long time, but look where you are now. And you've done it all yourself.

Josie could feel sweat sliding down into the armpits of her top, the thin silk fabric sticking to her skin like a licked stamp. She regretted not having worn black and drew her elbows in tight towards her ribs, hoping that Tom wouldn't spot the spreading stains. She had worn this blouse, much like every other new item of clothing over the past few weeks, hoping that Tom might comment on how she looked; he hadn't so far.

Hey, Tom said.

Hey, she said, half-motioning to get up so that she squatted on the paving stones. Tom didn't sit down so she stood up fully, leaving her brother sitting on the ground with his remaining sandwich in his lap.

Aren't you going to introduce me? asked Paul.

This is Paul, Josie said, nudging Paul's arm so that he would shake hands with Tom. Paul didn't get up so instead he just waved, finishing his mouthful of sandwich.

Hi Paul, Tom said.

Tom and I work together, Josie ventured.

Yeah, Tom agreed. Josie waited for him to say something else about how they knew each other, how else they might be connected, but he didn't. She scanned his face for any kind of reaction but he wore the same calm expression that he always did. His face appeared so smooth and open that it seemed to Josie that he could never have looked the way he did the night before, scrunched with a concentration that almost looked painful. She could feel a flush rising across her clavicles and up her neck. It had happened, she reminded herself, there was no way she could have a reaction like that if it hadn't happened.

It's good to see where she does all her important work, Paul said through a mouthful of crust, mimicking frantic typing with his hands. Josie noticed that his fingernails were dark with dirt as if they had been outlined in graphite pencil. She glanced at Tom to see if he had noticed but he made no sign; his gaze kept returning to the restaurant on the other side of the square.

The offices aren't quite as exciting on the inside, I'm afraid, Tom said.

Well, you're lucky to have her, Paul said. I bet she's brilliant.

Paul, Josie said.

Well. Sure, Tom said. Where are you from, by the way? South Africa? Cool accent.

Guernsey, Paul said, his eyebrow twitching with confusion.

Cool, Tom said again with a curt nod. Josie thought how Tom never usually described anything as cool, how he'd never normally repeat a word or phrase that he'd already used in conversation in case it came up dotted like a grammar error in Microsoft Word. The care he typically took with his speech had been a sign, Josie had long thought, of intelligence. His lack of care now felt cruel.

So, Paul from Guernsey, right? Pleasure to meet you.

Cool, Paul repeated back at him. Nice to see who my sister's hanging around with these days.

Tom stared at him. Great, he said.

Are you off for lunch somewhere nice, then? asked Josie.

Yeah, the Italian. Just with some friends, Tom replied, his eyes on her before settling on Paul again.

She wondered which friends they were, whether they were hers too, or had been until now. She had always considered Tom to be one of her best friends but now he was looking over her shoulder as if she was barely there at all.

Speak later, Tom said to Josie, for the second time that day.

She watched him march across the square and through the dark glass doors of the restaurant. She imagined him ordering a bottle of wine, Muscadet or Viognier, nonchalantly pouring it with one hand into the glasses of his friends while recounting some story. She knew the sound of his laugh so well that it was easy to picture their reactions to his skit about seeing Josie with some bloke with dirty fingernails called Paul, talking with his mouth full and picking out his tomatoes. Perhaps Tom would be telling anecdotes about the night before too, about how she'd stumbled on the front step into the building or been too dry. She had heard him talk before of other girls he had slept with, how this one vacation schemer had had flaps large enough for tent pegs, and how he had scrutinised the photos of a partner's husband on the wall while he bent her over the couch in her office. Josie had always been the one to tell him to shut up but had giggled along just the same, always keen to make Tom feel that his jokes were funny. She felt stupid now for expecting that because they were friends beforehand, he would treat her differently; she should have realised that women are not so different from one another in the eyes of a certain type of man.

Is that, like, your boyfriend then? joked Paul.

Josie shook her head. She picked up the box with its remaining scraps of salad. The coral crayfish tails were shining in the heat, the French dressing soaking into greasy grey blotches on the bottom of the cardboard tray.

He has such a rod up his arse.

He doesn't, she said faintly.

Oh come on, he said, elbowing her so that the rocket teetered off her fork. 'Cool accent'? What was that? What's his accent, even; who talks like that in real life?

You don't know him.

Does coke on Fridays and is shagging a senior partner, he said. And his secretary.

He's really not like that.

Who irons his shirts then?

She put her lunch down in her lap and squeezed her eyes shut.

Baby sister, he said, calm down. I'm only having you on.

Paul reached towards her, whether to hug her or pinch her, she didn't know, but she smacked his hands away. Why do you have to ruin everything?

Hey, what's up? I'm only teasing, you know me. What's the matter?

Josie said nothing, turning away from Paul. She thought of the night before, how she had squirmed around Tom's bed with her mouth feeling swollen and hair greasy with sweat. He owned his own apartment in Wapping, a fifth-floor new-build with engineered oak flooring and grey-grouted tiles; everything was precise and elegantly shelved, and expensive. He didn't have many books or photos or things. Her handbag had looked out of place on the kitchen sideboard, even though she had spent more money on it than any other wearable thing she owned. When she took herself off in a minicab in the weak hours of the morning, her handbag and bra and shoes bundled in her arms, it was as if she had tidied herself away. In one day, she had gone from best friend to lover to a lunchtime joke. The realisation amazed her. She could imagine feigned surprise on her housemate's face when she told her later that evening what happened with Tom. She could picture her expression because it was one that she had inadvertently made to her friends on numerous occasions. She didn't know what was worse, the humiliation of being rejected or the fact that she had let it happen at all.

You never told him that you had a brother, Paul said. Did you?

She couldn't remember which lies she had told to whom any more. Her glassy world was full of people trying to impress each other, and she had known ever since university that strategic socialising was just as important for getting ahead as anything else. Buying the right kind of clothes, claiming to like the right kind of wine and whisky: it all added up. She didn't think that she had categorically lied to Tom about Paul, but she knew that she would never have volunteered her brother's existence in conversation; pretending that he didn't exist would have been simpler than lying about what he was like, and what their life had been like, and about her dad.

I don't know, she said.

You don't know. So you didn't?

She didn't want to admit it, so she shrugged. Only as she was doing so did she realise it was more hurtful to dismiss the fact she'd lied than to own it.

Paul had always been on Josie's side. When their parents started arguing and their dad began drinking, Paul used to make them dens under the dining-room table or with the dog behind the sofa. He had bought her birthday cakes throughout her teenage years and kept the white striped candles in the kitchen drawer especially. Later, Paul was the one who cleaned up their dad's sick when he had incapacitated himself, or drove to pick him up from the brightness of the Accident and Emergency wing. Paul engaged with their dad so that she didn't have to. When she was seventeen, Paul had beaten up some pissed tourist in a kebab shop who wouldn't leave her alone, telling her to stand outside until he was done with him, and then Paul took her home in a cab, the bloke's blood red like ketchup down the front of his T-shirt.

The only time that Josie could remember her brother being truly angry with her was when she had zipped herself into the empty black cover of his surfboard, pretending that it was a body bag and she a corpse, holding her breath until her face lost its colour and he found her; when he did, ripping open the zip so fretfully he broke its teeth, he had screamed and screamed. Paul was silent now, but she could sense the same fury as when he'd dragged her out of the polyester casing and knelt down beside her, ready to do CPR, and she had started to giggle. She couldn't explain at the time why she had done it, no matter how much he asked her what she was playing at. She knew her rationale this time but felt too ashamed to say.

I should let you get back to work, said Paul, standing up. He brushed the crumbs from the thighs of his trousers as if they were her excuses.

I can stay a bit longer if you like, Josie said. You could tell me more about your course?

No, it's fine, he said, crumpling up his rubbish and casting his gaze around for a litter bin. You have a lot to be getting on with. I know you're busy, you did say you only had time for a quick lunch.

I'm not that busy actually, I don't have any meetings later—

It's fine. Glad I got to see you for a bit. Dad'll be pleased to know that we met up too. He sends his love.

Okay, she said.

He always does, you know, said Paul. Even when you don't pick up.

He walked with her as far as the entrance to the Underground station, and shrugged off the idea of coming up to see her office. She explained that the view was amazing but he said that he didn't need to see it. She couldn't determine whether the wobbly feeling in her sinuses and stomach was from guilt or relief. They hugged and he kissed her on the cheek, and she was struck by the distinct smell of surfboard wax on his clothes, sweet and balmy. She hadn't remembered that such a smell even existed. Saturday mornings spent squeaking out of damp wetsuits and untangling kelp from her hair. Bacon rolls and brick-brown tea from the kiosk. Paul hassling his mates to look away while she changed behind the open passenger door of his car, and the time she'd caught one of them watching her as she shucked the neoprene from her bare shoulders. She had felt the thrill then of what it was like to be looked at differently. When she'd left the island, after a summer of begging Tricky not to tell Paul about the relationship that had somehow washed up between them, Tricky had accused Josie of being a fake. The feeling of loss she experienced then felt as real as it did now, salt in her eyes like seawater and home very far away.

Paul stepped out of the embrace, hitching the straps of his backpack straight.

Paul, she said. He waited.

She squeezed his arm and he looked down at the grimy concrete floor that was splattered with chewing gum and bird droppings, his hand waving away the words she wasn't saying.

I'll see you at Christmas, he said. Love you.

She watched him descend the escalator until he disappeared out of sight, and then she turned back outside into the midday sun. The square was rustling with people, the sunlight coruscating on sushi packaging and water bottles. Nobody was watching her. The seagulls were crying from the buildings above and she turned her face up to listen. She supposed that Tom would be at lunch still. She thought how easy it was to tell the people who didn't care about you how much you liked them.

She took out her mobile phone and scrolled to the Guernsey landline number still filed under 'H' for 'Home'; a grey granite house on the south-westerly coast where Paul lived with their father. The rooms were cold in all seasons, so they'd always spent summers out in the steep strip of a garden that was overgrown with bindweed and cow parsley. On a good day like this, her father would be sitting on the front step with the sun on his face and his eyes on the sea. She dialled the number and waited.

Acknowledgements

First and foremost, thank you to the team at Felicity Bryan Associates – especially my agent, Carrie Plitt, for her honesty and constancy.

To Anna Kelly, for the care and enthusiasm with which she has approached these stories. To Nithya Rae, for her precision and patience. And to everyone at Virago who has helped to produce, package and promote the book.

To Declan Meade and Danny Denton at *The Stinging Fly*, for publishing an earlier version of *Good for a Laugh*, and Dan Bolger, for his editorial guidance.

To Jerwood Arts and the Arvon Foundation, and to David Eldridge, whose frank and kind mentoring wholly changed my approach to writing. I am forever grateful for having met Ian Dudley, Holly Corfield Carr, Deborah Stevenson and Grahame Williams, among others, at The Hurst.

With thanks to early readers of these stories for their invaluable advice and questions, including: Tom Campion, Alex

Christofi, Daisy Johnson and Laura Langlois. To Thomas Martin, whose dramaturgical guidance on the play *Rock* also influenced Annie's story here.

There are many wonderful people whose broader support and encouragement has kept me going during the writing of this book. They include: Beth, Charlotte and Tasha, and Alice and Jess; Helen; the Pembroke women, with special thanks to Sarah-Jane, and also to Jenn and Veronica for Canary Wharf fact-checking; Indira and Rhiannon; Charlie; David.

Thank you to my parents and my sister.